MARIANNE

MISS WOLFRASTON'S LADIES BOOK 1

JENNY HAMBLY

DEDICATION

To Dave,
You're there in all my books - honest!

CHAPTER 1

iss Wolfraston's Seminary for Young Ladies was a very select establishment. Not only did it promise to endow its young ladies with all the accomplishments a parent could wish for without any danger of them acquiring a surfeit of knowledge they could have little need of, but it refused to open its hallowed portals to any of the many wealthy families whose fortunes were made in trade and who wished their daughters to rub shoulders with other young ladies who were not so tainted. Thus, parents who had little interest in overseeing the education of their offspring, and did not wish for the inconvenience of having them underfoot or hiring a governess, could happily send their daughters away without any qualms of conscience and for only an additional four guineas, they could leave them to the tender care of Miss Wolfraston all year round, if they so desired.

That Miss Wolfraston's brother, who was in trade, had purchased the large establishment just outside

Bath for her could in no way detract from the acknowledged quality of the seminary. Indeed, the elegant deportment and modest manners displayed by the young ladies when they made their entrance into society marked them immediately as one of Miss Wolfraston's girls. They could confidently sally forth and impress the world at large with their accomplishments, and then promptly forget all about them once they had snared a husband.

Three of the oldest of these young ladies shared a large room in the east wing of the Palladian mansion. Each had recently attained their seventeenth birthday and if they had not already learned sufficiently well the accomplishments necessary to every young woman in search of a husband, it was unlikely that they would.

It might be expected that the bond of age and close confinement might draw them together into an intimate friendship, and this was certainly true of two of the young ladies. Miss Marianne Montagu, a dark beauty, was kind, lively, and intelligent and a foil to her friend Miss Charlotte Fletcher, who was fair, shy, and retiring.

The third occupant of the room, Lady Georgianna Voss, was unusually tall but fortunately was not attended by the slight awkwardness that sometimes hampered young ladies who suffered such an affliction. She made no effort to hide the fact; if anything she accentuated it by piling her plentiful ebony locks high upon her head and carrying herself in a very upright and proud manner. Benefiting from perfectly symmetrical features and a flawless complexion, she might have outshone both Marianne and Charlotte if it were not for the sullen pout that too often graced her rosebud mouth. She maintained an air of utmost superiority at all times, rarely unbending enough to share a moment of humour or a snippet of gossip. She was far more likely to drop an acidic comment into their conversation, her bite only matched by her undoubted wit.

The vagaries of their characters might have been explained by their differing backgrounds. Lady Georgianna came of very good stock and had had this fortunate fact drummed into her almost since the hour of her birth. Her father, the Earl of Westbury, could trace his ancestry back to before the Norman Conquest and was justly proud of such a lineage.

Her mother was an accredited beauty; unfortunately, this much-to-be-desired asset was matched only by her vanity. She had been quite content to have her daughter educated by a superior governess at home until she had threatened to match, if not outshine her, in looks. It was fortunate for her peace of mind that an acquaintance had mentioned Miss Wolfraston's fine seminary to her, thus enabling her to remove the daughter – who was a constant reminder of her receding youth – from her immediate vicinity without appearing the cold-hearted creature she undoubtedly was.

It was hardly surprising that Lady Georgianna, whose governess had not failed to provide her with a very good education, found herself with nothing to learn at Miss Wolfraston's seminary, apart from the art of pleasing conversation perhaps; for not having benefited from the warmth of human kindness, she did not know how to make herself agreeable to others.

Charlotte was quite in awe of her. Having been orphaned not long after her twelfth birthday, she had fallen under the care of her father's heir and successor, her cousin Lord Seymore. As a single young man he could not be expected to know how to go on with a girl of such tender years. He had sent her off to Miss Wolfraston's seminary and happily paid the extra sum required to keep her there all year round, although he did visit three times a year to see how she went on, and sent her very generous presents on her birthday and at Christmas.

Marianne was the daughter of Sir Frederick Montagu. He had a fondness for his daughter and had adored her mother. It was this affection that had led him to eventually remarry. He had become increasingly aware that Marianne and his long wished for son, who had been born only hours before his wife's death, lacked the gentle guiding hand that only a female could provide.

Not expecting to ever find anyone the equal of his dear departed wife, he had not perhaps been as discriminating as he could have been. Marianne's stepmother had appeared at first to dote on her new stepdaughter, but this fondness had waned not long after she was installed at Harwich Court. Finding Marianne to be disconcertingly independent and opinionated, and having an undesirable amount of influence over her father, she had wasted no time in persuading him it would be in Marianne's best interests to go to school where she would benefit from the society of other young ladies, and add some much needed polish to her alarmingly open manners before she made her come out.

Marianne had not objected; she found she could not bear to have her mother's place usurped by a woman who was so much her inferior and, with a maturity beyond her years, had realised that her continued presence could only cut up her father's peace.

As was their custom after dinner, these three ladies sat in the parlour that had been set aside for their personal use. As the summer break was fast approaching they each had much to think about.

"Will your cousin finally take you home this time?" Marianne said gently to her friend.

Charlotte's needle hovered above the sampler she was sewing and her shoulders slumped a little. "He did mention that he must look about for a companion for me, but I am not sure I set much store by it."

"He cannot leave you here forever," Lady Georgianna said dryly. "I do not know how you have borne staying here all year round, it is so very dull. He must be very selfish and heartless."

"I do not think him heartless, he is always very pleasant when he visits. I think he feels that I am happy here."

"And have you told him otherwise?" Lady Georgianna asked haughtily.

"Oh no," Charlotte admitted softly. "At first I was very unhappy, but that was to be expected after losing Mama and Papa so suddenly, but then Miss Hayes came and she was so kind and understanding I began to feel better. Indeed, it will be very strange not to live here now. I must admit I find the thought a little daunting."

"I am sure he will find you a splendid companion

and launch you into society. I very much hope we will make our come out together, next year," Marianne said encouragingly.

Charlotte's shoulders hunched a little more but she gave a tremulous smile. "I hope so too. It will be much less terrifying if you are there to support me."

"What on earth is there to be terrified of?" Lady Georgianna said with some asperity. "You have learnt how to talk, walk, sew, dance, and play, if very little else, and you are pretty enough. If you would but learn to overcome your shyness I am sure you will take."

Marianne cast her a rather exasperated glance. "I think you will find, Georgianna, that shyness is not something you can shed as you would a cloak."

Lady Georgianna raised her delicately arched brows. "It is all a question of resolution, surely?"

Charlotte sent her a timid glance. "Is there nothing you are afraid of?"

Lady Georgianna looked at Charlotte as if surprised she had dared to ask the question, her brows lowering slowly until her smooth brow creased into a frown. For a moment it seemed she would not deign to answer, but as the enquiring gazes of her companions turned away with a look of disappointment, she said so softly they had to lean towards her to catch her words, "Yes. Being forced to marry the Earl of Wedmore."

Their mouths dropped open in a most unladylike manner, as surprised that she had seen fit to confide in them as they were at the information received.

"You do not like him?" Charlotte asked gently.

Lady Georgianna gave a harsh little laugh. "I have

been informed that my liking or not liking him has no bearing on the matter. He is wealthy, of good family, and has an unimpeachable reputation. That he is also forty if he is a day, fat as a faun, and as dull as ditch-water, can in no way outweigh these sterling qualities."

"Surely you can refuse his offer," Charlotte exclaimed, horrified by the image these words had conjured.

"My parents are set on the match," Georgianna replied flatly. "They wish me to marry him before I even have a season so he can have no rival in my *affections*."

A mischievous glint came into Marianne's deep brown eyes. "Surely all that is required, Georgianna, is a little resolution?"

Lady Georgianna's icy glance turned sharply towards Marianne. Charlotte held her breath, admiring the audacity of her friend but sure a scathing response would be forthcoming.

But on seeing an intelligent humour rather than spite gleaming in the eyes that boldly held her own, a reluctant grin twitched her lips, and then she laughed.

"Touché," she acknowledged. "I deserved that I suppose."

"Could you not appeal to your mother, at least?" Marianne felt certain that her own would never have forced her into such a situation.

The rare humour that had briefly lit Lady Georgianna's deep blue eyes quickly faded. She shook her head. "The sooner I am off her hands the happier she will be."

The door to the parlour opened on her words. A very neat lady glided into the room. Her movements were marked by the grace and elegance that she had been employed to teach to others. Her rich auburn hair was pinned ruthlessly atop her head and she regarded the young ladies with wide set green eyes, a faint smile on her generous lips.

"Stop slouching, Charlotte," she said gently. "I cannot recall how many times I have assured you that hunching your shoulders like that will not make you disappear but only ensure you stand out more once you enter society."

"Yes, Miss Hayes." She straightened her spine immediately, more out of a desire to please her favourite teacher than any chagrin she might have felt at the rebuke.

Next, her gaze travelled to the young lady sitting in the window seat. "Lady Georgianna, you will find that book much easier to read if you turn it the right way up."

Marianne covered her mouth with her hand to hide her smile when she felt those eagle eyes turn in her direction.

"Marianne, were you intending to embroider a squirrel onto your reticule or your initials? If it is the latter, you have failed miserably and must start again."

That young lady, far from being mortified, glanced down at the scrap of material discarded in her lap and stifled a giggle, her humour reflected in Miss Hayes' eyes.

"Now, girls, I am afraid that due to Miss Wolfraston being a trifle indisposed today, it has only just come to my attention that each of you received a letter this morning."

Marianne and Charlotte got to their feet at once,

but Lady Georgianna remained where she was with a marked lack of enthusiasm, forcing Miss Hayes to cross the room to deliver it.

"I will give you time to read them but then you must all retire; it has been a long day, and I am too tired to sit up this evening."

When Miss Hayes had left the room, Marianne said, "As this is an evening for confidences, what say we share our news? You complain of it all being so dull here, Georgianna, so let us take it in turns to read our letters."

Lady Georgianna shrugged. "If it will please you, but I warn you, I doubt very much that mine will have anything interesting to entertain you."

Marianne smiled at her. She had not warmed to Georgianna, but this evening's revelations had given her pause for thought. It was a shame it had taken almost until the end of the year for her to unbend a little, but she now realised that behind that cold façade lay vulnerability. It was she realised, their common bond.

"You go first, Charlotte," she said. "I imagine your letter is from Lord Seymore?"

Charlotte looked a little bemused. "No. I do not recognise the hand, but it is far too elegant for it to be his."

Marianne looked intrigued. "Well, who else writes to you?"

"No one," Charlotte said. "My only other blood relative lives in India and I have heard nothing from Great Aunt Augusta for years."

Lady Georgianna began to look a little interested.

She left the window seat and came closer to the fire that had burned low in the grate.

"Well go on then, open it." She perched on the edge of the sofa next to Marianne.

Charlotte broke the seal and began to scan the letter.

"No, no." Marianne wagged an admonishing finger. "That is cheating. You must not leave us in such suspense."

"Oh, of course not." She cleared her throat a little self-consciously. "*My dearest Charlotte, I really cannot believe you have already celebrated your seventeenth birthday. You must think I am completely heartless to have been so remiss in writing to you for such a long time. I have no excuse but will say this, when you are older time seems to fly by at three times the rate it does when you are but a child. But, amazing as this seems to me, you are a child no longer. Lord Seymore wrote to me some time ago for advice on when and how to bring you out, only I had already left India and the letter and I crossed paths somewhere on the journey. It has finally found me however, and I was never more mortified than when I discovered that my poor departed niece's only child had grown up in a school! Men are such thoughtless creatures! Well, I have had words with your cousin and you will stay there no longer. We are at present at our estate near Dorchester, and Lord Carstairs and I are quite in agreement that you must come to us as soon as it may be arranged. I have also sent Miss Wolfraston a letter informing her of this development, as has Lord Seymore. So, my child, pack up your things and prepare to be welcomed back into the bosom of your family. Yours affectionately, Your Great Aunt Augusta.*"

Charlotte read the words in a colourless tone, almost as if she were reading one of her lessons from a dry history book. Indeed, the contents of the letter seemed to her as unlikely as many of the tales she had read.

Marianne, who had always had an excellent imagination, imbued them with the fond tones of a doting eccentric, wreathed in volumes of exotic muslin, a magnificent turban upon her head. Leaning forwards she grasped Charlotte's hands in her own.

"But this is wonderful!" she said, smiling. "Your great aunt sounds quite wonderful, Charlotte. You are to have a home, at last!"

Even Lady Georgianna offered a small smile. "This is good news indeed, Charlotte. Please accept my congratulations. I have come to realise that to be cast out of one's home is not at all comfortable. That you have suffered this inconvenience for so long without a word of complaint is as commendable as it is outrageous."

"Thank you, Georgianna," Charlotte said softly before turning to Marianne. "It is your turn next, I think. Is it from your papa?"

"Yes." Marianne smiled, unfolding her missive. "But I warn you, Papa sometimes rambles a bit. *Dear Marianne, I hope you are well and happy. It is very strange not to have you near. I frequently look up half expecting to see you curled up on the sofa in my study with your nose in a book. Your brother is well and has taken to riding like a duck to water. I should not be surprised, you were just the same. I was so looking forward to seeing you this summer, but I must put aside my selfish longings for I have some exciting news for you. Your Aunt Fanny paid us a visit last week. She has decided that she wishes to try the waters at Cheltenham as she has heard many good things about the resort and she is not feeling quite the thing (obviously that is not the exciting bit). Well, where was I? Oh, yes.*

She has requested that you join her for she is certain you will enjoy it having been assured that there are many amusements to be found there, and it will give you a chance to experience society a little before you make your official come out next season. She has indicated that you may take a friend with you if you so desire, as she cannot guarantee she will always have the energy required to fully entertain you and cannot dispense with the attentions of her companion, Miss Bragg. If you do not wish to go, you must of course come home. But I must admit, she did seem a little low, and I am sure your mother would have wished you to offer your support to her only sister. You are always such a ray of sunshine that I am sure that a week in your company will do her far more good than any amount of water from the spas there. I remain your affectionate Papa."

"Well, it would seem today is a day for surprises," said Georgianna. "Will you go?"

"Oh yes." Marianne smiled. "Aunt Fanny is very kind. But since my uncle died she has now and then a fit of the dismals. In truth, she has turned into something of a hypochondriac. I suppose her latest doctor has recommended the waters at Cheltenham. It will do her good to get out and about, at all events. She used to be very gay but has been living in a very quiet way since she was widowed."

Lady Georgianna slowly unfolded her letter, a ghost of a smile curving her lips. "I do hope it is not one of my aunts inviting me for a visit. They are both crusty and very demanding. I would rather remain here than suffer that fate. *Georgianna, I am afraid I must do without you for a little longer. Your brother is not at all well. The doctor assures me that he is in no danger but he has a bad case of chincough, and as it is contagious, it would not be wise for you to come to us just yet. I had invited Lord Wedmore to a small house party to mark your homecoming and have had to postpone it. It is most vexing! Mama.*"

Lady Georgianna sat looking down at her letter for a moment, her face stony. "It seems I am to stay here after all."

"No, you shall not," said Marianne.

Lady Georgianna's dull eyes flickered towards her.

"Aunt Fanny said I might bring a friend, did she not?"

A flash of surprise momentarily brightened her face. "Mama will never permit it," Georgianna said quietly.

"Leave it to me." Marianne covered her neatly crossed hands with her own. "You do not know Aunt Fanny. She is far too lazy to enjoy writing letters, which is why I received her invitation through Papa, but she can be *very* persuasive. She made an extremely good marriage to the Earl of Brancaster, who moved in the most select circles. I will write to her immediately and explain your case. She *will* persuade your mother, I am certain."

Lady Georgianna gave a rather wan smile. "I may not know your Aunt Fanny, but I do know my mother. But thank you, it is a kind thought."

The door opened on her words and Miss Hayes again came into the room.

"Miss Hayes, am I really to go to Great Aunt Augusta for the summer?" Charlotte's voice was full of doubt.

"Indeed you are, what is more, I am to go with you, my dear."

"Oh, I am so glad," Charlotte cried, jumping to her feet. "But how? Why?"

"Charlotte, do try for a little decorum please." Her words were softened by the smile that lurked in her eyes. "Your great aunt has been very busy on your behalf. It appears you have mentioned my name to your cousin on more than one occasion and he, in turn, mentioned it to your great aunt. She and her husband knew my grandfather, Lord Beaumont, and she claims she met me when I was a child, although I do not recall it. She has requested that I not only bring you to her, but that I stay as your companion for the summer."

Lady Georgianna hurried out of the room, a stricken look on her face and her eyes suspiciously bright. Miss Hayes' presence was the one thing that might have made her stay bearable.

CHAPTER 2

I t was a glorious summer's day. The sun streamed down onto the long, hard-baked road of Cheltenham High Street. The clement weather had ensured that the many visitors to the ever-growing spa town were out in force. A variety of equipages, equestrians, and pedestrians thronged the wide thoroughfare.

It was hard to believe that before the discovery of the mineral waters, a more retired, rural, and unfrequented place would have been difficult to find. Then, the High Street had been distinguished by a stream running down the centre of the road, with conveniently placed, uneven stepping stones for the small populace to hop across if they wished to visit the few modest establishments that it possessed. Now, it was lined with very tasteful shops, boarding houses, and inns. It also offered three circulating libraries and two assembly rooms for the entertainment of its visitors. Elegant squares and a most superior crescent had been built within the last few years and although it was not as established as Bath, it was second only to it in this part of the country.

A smart curricle driven by an extremely stylish gentleman weaved its way amongst the throng.

"Remind me again, Bamber, why did I agree to come with you to this infernal place? I am sure it will be filled with dyspeptic old men, or worse, bored females of indeterminate age with nothing better to do than take the waters to cure themselves of their imagined ailments."

The other occupant of the vehicle, Sir Horace Bamber, who had been happily nodding and smiling at one or two acquaintances they had passed, swivelled his shoulders the better to survey his companion without any danger of poking his eye with his splendidly high shirt points. It was a testament to the quality of his valet that even the heat of the sun had not thus far managed to wilt them.

"I say, Cranbourne, don't malign it until you have tried it. Dear old King George himself came here in 1788, don't you know?"

Lord Cranbourne glanced briefly in his direction, a glimmer of amusement disturbing his habitually bored gaze. "I am aware, Bamber, but look what happened to him!"

"Yes, well, the less said about that the better. You came, dear chap, because beneath your baleful glare and haughty exterior, you're a damned fine fellow."

Rather than looking flattered by this generous encomium, Lord Cranbourne looked positively revolted.

"Well you are," Sir Horace insisted. "Couldn't have driven meself with this plaguey gout, that's for certain. What's more, you've saved me from a dashed awkward situation." His face fell for a moment, and he said in a voice of doom, "Mother's matchmaking again. This time she's invited some distant cousin of mine for a few weeks. Anne, I think, or is it Jane? Haven't seen her for an age but I do remember she prattles non-stop, has buckteeth, and a squint! Mother can assure me all she likes that she is much improved, but I'm not fool enough believe her."

Lord Cranbourne flicked his whip and his horses shot between a farmer's cart and an oncoming carriage with only inches to spare. "Whilst you have my sympathy, Bamber, if you are labouring under the charming but misguided belief that I have come only on your behalf, rid yourself of it."

"Then why did you come?"

Lord Cranbourne expertly guided his equipage under the arch that led to the yard of The George Inn. "I am not at all sure, my good fellow. Let us call it a whim, if you please."

"I may not be up to every rig and row in town, Cranbourne, but I'm not such a knock in the cradle that I will swallow that line. There's something lurking at the edges of my memory, now what is it?" he mused.

"Leave it lurking," advised Lord Cranbourne.

Sir Horace climbed down from the curricle rather awkwardly, careful not to put any undue weight on his left foot. "I've got it by Jupiter!" he suddenly exclaimed, delighted to have found the elusive recollection. "Maria! Your sister has invited herself down to Cranbourne this summer. Yes, she told me all about it at Lady Sudsbury's ball. The thing is, I was only listening with half an ear."

"You are to be commended on your fortitude," Lord Cranbourne said dryly, tossing a coin to the stable lad and striding towards the inn.

"Yes, well, she does rattle on a trifle," admitted Sir Horace. "Said she had invited the Ponsonby chit down for a small house party." He leaned heavily on his cane as he limped after his friend.

He came to a sudden standstill, his eyes widening as comprehension finally dawned. "You devil! You've bolted, Cranbourne! You can't do that! Not at all the thing to hold a house party and not be present!"

"Ah," his friend said softly. "But then it is not my house party, it is Maria's."

It was fortunate that Sir Horace had had the fore-sight to reserve a private parlour, as the landlord assured them that he was full to bursting.

"Well, this is not so bad is it?" Sir Horace lowered himself onto a comfortable sofa and carefully lifted his foot onto the footstool that had been thoughtfully placed in front of it. "Now, where was I?"

Lord Cranbourne leant back in his chair and sipped the glass of wine that had been provided for his refreshment. "This is quite tolerable," he said, having no wish to resume their former conversation.

But Sir Horace was not to be so easily put off. "House party, Ponsonby chit! You could do worse, you know, Cranbourne. Fine looking gal, good family and all that."

"But with a laugh that could shatter glass," Lord Cranbourne murmured.

"Oh, you are too nice in your requirements," his

friend protested. "I thought you might make a match of it with Lady Anne Richmond last season. You cannot deny that she had grace, elegance, and beauty. She certainly seemed very taken with you."

Lord Cranbourne crossed one long, muscled leg over the other and seemed to become quite fascinated with his glossy hessian boots. "Taken with the prospect of spending my fortune, I think you will find."

"Well you can hardly blame her for that, old fellow. Never met a female yet who wouldn't relish the thought of spending a fortune if she could but lay her hands on one, after all. What is it you want in a wife anyway?"

Lord Cranbourne looked pensive. "I cannot tell you. I only know that I have not yet found it in any of the many and varied ladies of my acquaintance." He gave a dry laugh. "Perhaps they might be more appealing if they showed as much interest in me as they did in my prospects."

Sir Horace had been half reclining in a most slovenly way, but he suddenly shot upright as he was struck by a blinding revelation, his green eyes brightening with rare animation.

"By Jove, Cranbourne, I would never have believed it of you! You are a romantic!"

Lord Cranbourne's lips twisted into a sneer. "Don't be any more of a fool than you can help, Bamber. I don't think any of my past connections would apply that particular epithet to me."

Sir Horace chuckled with unimpaired good humour. "Now, now, Cranbourne, no need for that tone. Haven't I known you almost since we were in leading strings? Your secret's safe with me. Anyway, I wasn't referring to your ladybirds. Come to think of it, why you would worry about someone only wanting you for your money is beyond me; you must have spent a fortune on the last one. Every time I saw her she had some new bauble around her neck!"

"She has had her last," he said a little grimly. "She was as greedy as she was beautiful, but at least she had the merit of never pretending to be interested in anything else."

Sir Horace suddenly looked uncomfortable. He clapped his hand to his head. "Blast my wretched memory. I had forgotten Melissa!"

"I suggest you forget her again," his friend said softly.

"Well, I'll try, old chap. But that's the problem with memories; can't catch one when you need to, and when you are least expecting it, one suddenly pops into your head and you can't get rid of it!"

Lord Cranbourne closed his eyes wearily. The image of a tall, graceful creature, with golden hair and laughing blue eyes swam into his mind. He had been barely more than a stripling when he had fallen for Melissa Gordan seven years ago, and he had fallen hard. She had encouraged him at every turn, calling him by his first name when they were private, and allowing him to steal a kiss or two on a dark balcony outside a crowded ballroom. However, when he had proposed to her she had turned him down without a moment's thought.

"Oh, Anthony," she had laughed. "I cannot! You must see that I cannot. You are only a second son!"

The following day she had accepted a proposal from Lord Silchester, who may have been in his fifties, but had the distinction of being a marquis. They were married by special license within a matter of days.

Angry and disillusioned he had persuaded his father to buy him his colours, and had been on the point of setting off for Portugal when he found his situation cruelly reversed. Both his father and his brother had contracted a fever and were dead within a week. He had returned to Cranbourne as the earl.

"Oh, where is my bonnet?" Charlotte looked frantically about her. "I must not keep Miss Hayes waiting!"

"Here it is, you goose." Georgianna had been helping her pack, unable to watch her hopelessly disorganised attempts to achieve the feat. She retrieved it from the floor and dusted it off briskly.

Charlotte smiled her thanks as she took it. As she put it on, a small package wrapped in paper fell to the floor. "What is this?"

"It is nothing," Georgianna said, colouring slightly. "A mere trifle."

Marianne put down the chemise she had been folding and came over to her friends.

"Open it, then. You will not discover what it is merely by looking at it!"

Charlotte carefully unwrapped it and found a small sketch set inside a painted card frame. It was a portrait of herself, very accurately rendered, but she did not recognise the confident glint in her expression.

"It is wonderful." Tears filled her eyes.

"Do not be such a wet blanket, Charlotte," Georgianna said dryly. "It is to remind you how you will look when you overcome your shyness and become a little more sure of yourself. Practise that look in the mirror!"

Charlotte glanced at the drawing again and then attempted what she imagined was a fair imitation of the slightly autocratic look.

Marianne started to laugh and soon the others joined in. 'Y-you definitely n-need to practise," she gasped. "You looked as if you were in p-pain!"

There was a brief knock at the door and two servants came in closely followed by Miss Hayes. Once Charlotte's trunks had been removed, she smiled at the girls.

"I am glad to find you all in such high spirits but pray calm yourselves before Miss Wolfraston hears you, or she will soon be berating you for lowering the tone of this fine establishment!"

She waited for their gusts of laughter to fade away to the odd faint giggle before she continued.

"So, you all begin a new chapter. I am sure you will do very well but I expect you to write and let me know how you go on." She sent a sympathetic glance in Lady Georgianna's direction before shepherding Charlotte out of the room.

The laughter died with their departure. Marianne packed the last of her belongings into her trunk and firmly closed the lid. Her father was sending her other things directly to Cheltenham with her maid. Her carriage was already waiting but she had dawdled over her packing, somehow reluctant to leave her room-mate alone.

She sent a surreptitious glance in Lady Georgianna's direction. It seemed that her prediction that her mother would never allow her to visit Cheltenham with Marianne was to be proved correct. No letter had been forthcoming.

"I'm sure Lady Westbury will send for you before too long," she said gently. "And you will have the room all to yourself now. I remember how cross you were when you discovered you had to share."

Lady Georgianna grimaced. "Insufferable, wasn't I?"

"A bit," Marianne admitted with a twinkle.

Her friend gave a hard little laugh. "I will miss your honesty and your humour." She crossed the room to a squat set of drawers that fitted neatly under the window. She retrieved something and then crossed the room to Marianne, her hands behind her back.

"Perhaps this will make up for it." She reached out an arm, a very elegant reticule dangled from one tapering finger. It was fashioned from white silk and had a delicately embroidered pink rose surrounded by green foliage in its centre. Marianne's initials were set neatly below it.

Much to Georgianna's surprise, Marianne stepped forward and embraced her.

"Thank you," she said gently. "It is far superior to my ham-fisted attempt!"

"Ladies!"

They broke apart as they registered the disapproving tones of Miss Wolfraston. A small, plump lady with a hooked nose and small beady eyes stood in the doorway.

"Have I not taught you that it is very vulgar to show an excess of emotion?" she complained, coming into the room.

Marianne and Georgianna's eyes met briefly, a glimmer of laughter in both before they dropped their gaze to the floor.

"That is better. I hope that when you go into society you will remember that how you behave reflects directly on this seminary. Lady Georgianna, I have just this moment received a letter from Lady Westbury. It seems you are to go with Miss Montagu after all. I suggest she helps you pack for she is already late as it is."

"But that is wonderful," exclaimed Marianne.

"I am not at all sure it is wise," Miss Wolfraston said, dampeningly. "It is a shame you have only had the benefit of this school for two terms, Miss Montagu, for you often display a liveliness that is not at all pleasing. You would do well to observe Lady Georgianna closely and follow her lead, for she, I am pleased to say, always comports herself with reserve and dignity."

The girls flew into action the moment the door closed behind her.

"What a quiz!" Georgianna said, randomly grabbing armfuls of clothes and throwing them onto her bed, her penchant for organisation overridden by her desire to be gone from the school. "We have both only been here two terms, yet Miss Wolfraston will take all the credit for my perceived merits but accept none for your apparent failings!"

"Never mind Miss Wolfraston," grinned Marianne. "Get packing. Cheltenham and Aunt Fanny await us!"

CHAPTER 3

I t was late when they arrived in St George's Place. The house Aunt Fanny had hired was both elegant and commodious. Not liking to have strangers about her, she had brought her own servants who would understand her requirements without her having to explain them. Milton, her impressively regal butler, received them with a distant formality Miss Wolfraston would have approved of.

"Lady Georgianna, Miss Montagu," he greeted them in a low measured voice, offering them the slightest of bows. "Lady Brancaster is attending a ball at the lower assembly room this evening, but I shall send for her directly."

"Oh, do not disturb her on our account." Marianne smiled. "It has been a long day and I am sure a spot of supper and our beds is all that we require."

His already stiff posture seemed to become even more rigid, but before he could reply a door at the end of the long entrance hall opened, and a plump lady with a kindly face hurried towards them.

"There you are at last, my ladies," she smiled, dipping into a swift curtsy. "I'm Mrs Settle, my lady's housekeeper. You must be quite exhausted. I will show you to your rooms immediately and by the time you have tidied yourselves up a trifle, your supper will be ready."

A pained looked flitted across the butler's face for the briefest moment at Mrs Settle's unwarranted friendliness, but he merely nodded at her before moving away in a stately fashion.

"Don't you mind Milton," she said in hushed tones as they ascended the stairs. "He appears starched up but he's all right when you get to know him."

They had been placed in adjacent chambers. Both were large and airy and decorated in a light floral wallpaper. As Marianne opened the door to her room, her face broke into a wide smile as she saw a maid, only a few years older than herself arranging a few knick-knacks on her dressing table.

"Nancy!" Marianne hurried forwards and took the maid's hands. "How are you?"

"The happier for seeing you, miss," she smiled. "The court is not the same without you to brighten it up."

"And how is father and my brother?"

"All is well, miss, don't you fret. Your father is enjoying spending time with young Master Simon. He's as boisterous as any five year old boy should be."

Marianne quirked a brow. "And how does Lady Montagu like that?"

"Well enough," Nancy said. "She might have got rid of you for now, miss, but she knows better than to upset the apple cart by trying to drive a wedge between your father and Master Simon. Besides, with his angelic looks and winning smile, he has all but wound her round his very grubby little finger!"

Marianne laughed. "I am glad of it."

A light knock fell upon the door and Georgianna came into the room.

"Nancy, this is my friend Lady Georgianna Voss. Would you mind very much looking after both of us? Her own maid cannot come just yet as she is helping nurse her little brother, who is ill."

The maid curtsied. "It will be my pleasure, Lady Georgianna. As soon as I've unpacked the rest of Miss Montagu's things, I shall see to yours."

Georgianna nodded politely. "I would be most grateful. How should I address you? What is your last name?"

"It's Pugh, my lady."

"Oh, call her Nancy," Marianne said. "She has been with us since she was a girl and I could not change the habit of calling her by her first name when she became my maid."

"Yes, please do," the maid smiled. "It will be less confusing that way. Lady Montagu is the only one who calls me Pugh, and I cannot get used to it!"

Georgianna inclined her head. "Very well, Nancy. I could manage the simple styles we kept at school quite well on my own, but I will need some help if I am to appear a little more sophisticated now we are to go into wider society."

"Indeed you will, my lady. What a pretty pair you will make!"

"You are very lucky in your maid," Georgianna said softly as they descended the stairs. "I imagine you could confide in her. Stokes, my maid, is much older than I and frequently reports back to Mama. I am glad she is not here for she would be writing home at every opportunity to inform her of my every movement."

"Whatever for?" Marianne asked bemused. "You are always very correct and all that is dignified."

Georgianna shrugged. "I do not know. Although Mama has never wished to spend a great deal of time with me, she has always liked to know of my every achievement or failing."

"And what are these failings?" Marianne asked, intrigued.

"Mostly being outspoken. Having an opinion. And worst of all, not being afraid to voice it."

Marianne looked much struck by these revelations. "She is right. You are! You do!"

Lady Georgianna suddenly grinned and gently elbowed her friend in the ribs. "What is sauce for the goose—"

Marianne laughed. "I know, but the difference is, at my home it is not considered a failing!" Her smile slipped after a moment. "Or at least, it never used to be."

As they reached the bottom of the sweeping staircase, Milton came into the hall from the morning room that looked over the street and glided silently past them. He opened the front door and a slender lady, clothed in a dress of plain crape over a white satin slip, distinguished by a white velvet ribband thickly spangled with gold, almost fell over the threshold. Her amber India shawl, which had been negligently drawn through her arms, slipped to the floor as she put out a hand to regain her balance. Her fair hair was arranged artfully in dishevelled curls, confined with a white velvet band. She looked absurdly youthful for a lady somewhere in her mid thirties.

"Really, Milton," she complained, "you gave me such a shock. Miss Bragg had not even rung the bell yet. Have you been hovering there all evening?"

As he stooped to retrieve her shawl, she saw her visitors. Her slight frown disappeared and a wide smile transformed her expression from peevish to delighted in an instant.

"Marianne!" she said, rushing forwards and enveloping her in a scented embrace. "My darling girl! I am so glad you have come. It was quite ridiculous of Frederick to send you to school and so I told him. But then nothing that w——"

Suddenly remembering her other visitor, she thought better of whatever it was she had been going to say. "Well, never mind."

"I am so glad to finally see you out of mourning colours, Aunt," smiled Marianne. "You look quite wonderful."

Lady Brancaster gave a trill of laughter. "Don't be ridiculous, child, I am past the age of looking wonderful. But I am making an effort to pick up some of the threads of my old life. It has been nearly three years now since I was widowed, and my poor Samuel would not wish me to languish over his passing forever, after all."

"I am sure he would not," agreed Marianne.

"I couldn't face tackling the season, but I thought perhaps Cheltenham might be the perfect place to dip my toe into the waters again."

"As well as drink them!"

Lady Brancaster pulled a face. "Yes, they are positively disgusting, although I have been assured that they are far more palatable than those at Bath."

She turned to her other guest, her gaze sweeping over her assessingly. "You must be Lady Georgianna," she smiled. "How very tall you are. It is quite wonderful. Very striking. So elegant a figure too. I am very pleased you were able to come."

Any image that Lady Georgianna might have fostered of an ailing, frail creature, worn down by life's burdens, was firmly dispelled.

"I am honoured to be here, Lady Brancaster," Georgianna said. "I thought my mother had refused, but then the letter arrived at the very last moment."

"Yes, well, I'm sorry about that," Lady Brancaster said, a little sheepishly. "It took me a little while to get around to writing to Lady Westbury. But here you are, after all."

A diminutive lady, who had been hovering behind Lady Brancaster, cleared her throat.

"Oh there you are, Aurora. Do not stand there in the shadows but come and greet our guests."

At first glance, Miss Bragg was everything you might expect in a companion. She was of indeterminate age, dressed plainly, had mousy coloured hair, unremarkable looks, and was by nature quiet. Only the twinkle that often lurked in her pale grey eyes hinted at hidden depths.

"How are you, Miss Bragg?"

"Oh, I am doing tolerably well, thank you, Miss Montagu," she said softly. "How good of you to ask."

Lady Georgianna nodded politely. "I am pleased to make your acquaintance."

"And I yours, Lady Georgianna. Quite delighted. What a striking pair you make. Yes, indeed, very striking." She trailed off as if her thoughts were elsewhere.

"Supper is served," announced Milton in sonorous tones.

"Oh, you poor dears," exclaimed Lady Brancaster. "You must be famished. Come along and tell me all about Miss Wolfraston's seminary."

"I'll be with you in a moment," murmured Miss Bragg, mounting the stairs.

"Now," Lady Brancaster said, almost as soon as they were seated. "Tell me, Marianne, what have you learned that you did not know before?"

Marianne laughed. "I have learned that my sewing is even more execrable than I had imagined. Georgianna puts me to shame – hers is superb. I have also learned that I am too lively and so may well bring Miss Wolfraston's seminary into disrepute when I go into society."

Lady Brancaster sighed and shook her head. "What nonsense. Your liveliness is enchanting and sewing is overrated!"

Being very fond of her niece, she had jumped to her defence without thinking. But it now occurred to her that her comments might not appear flattering to Lady Georgianna. She sent her an apologetic glance.

"Not that your proficiency in the accomplishment is not a credit to you, Lady Georgianna. Marianne wrote that you too had not attended for very long, did you learn anything useful?"

"Yes," she replied quietly, her glance shifting to

Marianne. "I learned how intolerably toplofty I was and how pleasant it is to have a friend."

As Lady Brancaster was not at all sure how to answer this, it was perhaps fortunate that Miss Bragg came just then into the room. She carried a warm shawl.

"Here you are, my dear," she said to her employer, rushing forwards and draping it over her shoulders. "The amber one was perfect for a ball, but I think you will find this one far more practical for the house."

"Thank you, Aurora. I do not know what I would do without you. It would not do to take a chill when I have guests to entertain."

"Exactly so," agreed Miss Bragg. "I would not be surprised if two such striking looking girls set the town by its ears! I certainly do not think we can leave them to their own devices. Dear me, no, it wouldn't serve at all."

"I am sure you are right, Aurora," Lady Brancaster sighed. "It is just as well I am feeling more the thing."

"I must admit, Aunt Fanny, you appear remarkably well considering Papa suggested you were in the dismals," murmured Marianne.

If she had thought to discompose her aunt, she was to be disappointed. Lady Brancaster placed two dainty elbows on the table and dropped her chin into her cupped hands, a mischievous twinkle brightening her cornflower blue eyes.

"I may have exaggerated, just a little," she admitted.

Her expression suddenly darkened. "But that *woman* – I'm sorry my dear but I cannot bring myself to call her Lady Montagu, that title will always belong to my dear sister in my mind – was not at all of the opinion that you should come. She wanted all the kudos of introducing such an attractive girl into the *ton* herself next season, no doubt, for you are bound to be a hit you know, and even though she can have had nothing to do with the development of your character, disposition, or looks, she will not hesitate to take all the credit for them you can be sure. And you know how much your father likes a quiet life. If I hadn't laid it on a little thick he would never have consented. But your papa has a kind heart, and I was able to persuade him after all. Besides, I was feeling a little down pin, everything had become so very dull, and he could quite see that you would brighten my days."

"I will do my best," laughed Marianne.

"How did you persuade my mama?" Georgianna said curiously. It was a question she had asked herself many times on the way to Cheltenham.

Lady Brancaster looked at her pensively for a moment. "I know your mama, of old," she admitted. "We made our come out in the same season."

Georgianna surprised her hostess by giving a wry laugh. "She would not have liked that at all! Mama does not like competition."

A gurgle of laughter escaped Lady Brancaster. "I will take that as a compliment. I can see you are as astute as you are beautiful, Lady Georgianna. No wonder your mama sent you to school. You have inherited her looks, although your eyes are of an even deeper blue, I think. I would not have thought it possible, and then you are dark like your father whereas she is fair. You have his height too. It is a startling combination. I can quite see that it might be difficult for her to witness your blossoming just at the moment when her own looks are fading. Appearances have always been of prime importance with your mama."

"I know!" said Georgianna, a wealth of meaning encapsulated in those two short words. "But I am still at a loss as to how your persuaded her."

Lady Brancaster sat up and waved an arm as if in defeat. "Oh, keeping secrets is too wearisome, so I shall tell you, although I probably ought not. I may not have been completely truthful earlier—" She broke off as she registered her niece's sceptically raised brow. "Do not be impertinent, Marianne. Now where was I?"

"Not being completely truthful," Marianne murmured.

Her aunt sent her a quelling glance, although the dimple that peeped in her right cheek hinted that she was not really displeased. Turning her attention back to her niece's friend she said, "I wrote to Lady Westbury almost immediately but she refused."

"I thought she would."

"Girls!" Lady Brancaster said, half laughing, half exasperated. "If you keep interrupting you shall drive me to distraction!"

They exchanged a smile but held their peace. After a moment, Lady Brancaster continued.

"As I was saying, she refused. She indicated that Lady Georgianna was on the verge of making a very desirable connection and did not think it wise for her to be exposed to the masses before the knot was tied, so to speak."

Georgianna's lips twisted in distaste.

"Oh," breathed Lady Brancaster. "I can see you are not enamoured with the idea. I had not meant to ask so soon, but who is it?"

"The Earl of Wedmore."

"Oh, my poor, poor child. It will not do. Really it will not. He is, of course, respectable and very well to do, but so prosy and preachy. Whatever is Serena thinking of?"

"Perhaps you could use your remarkable powers of persuasion again on my behalf in the matter?" Georgianna said wryly.

Lady Brancaster looked thoughtful. "I do not promise anything, my dear, but I wouldn't be at all surprised if I came up with something! Anyway, I wrote to Lady Westbury again, expressing my disappointment and asking her to reconsider her decision."

It was Georgianna's turn to raise a sceptical brow. "And?"

A slight pink tinge crept into Lady Brancaster's cheeks. "I may have mentioned that if it got about, although I, of course, would not breathe a word, that she had preferred to leave her daughter alone at the seminary when she had had the opportunity to visit with friends, it would not reflect well on her."

Lady Georgianna looked at her in awe. "She would not have liked that!"

"No. But she would like to appear selfish and mean spirited even less."

CHAPTER 4

Used to the hours kept at the seminary, Marianne and Georgianna were up early. Even so, when they entered the morning room, they found Miss Bragg sat by the fireplace knitting and Lady Brancaster sipping a cup of chocolate, a dainty lace cap set atop her golden locks.

"Do not looked so surprised!" she laughed. "We do not keep town hours here, you know. I had meant to mention it last night, but what with one thing and another it quite slipped my mind. I am glad to see you are not slug-a-beds! Although there are now a few spas to choose from, I have been assured that the original well is still the best for someone of my delicate constitution. But it gets horribly crowded as the day wears on, so I like to go before breakfast. It is a pleasant walk and helps give me an appetite. After being shut up all day in a carriage yesterday, I am convinced you will both enjoy it."

It appeared she was not alone in her habits. There was already a steady stream of people strolling along the wide, clean pavements towards the church when they reached High Street. The houses that fronted onto the road, although not uniform in appearance, were pretty and well maintained, some of them boasting delicate wrought iron balconies, and the overall impression was charming. As they turned into the churchyard, they found a broad, commodious walk that was shaded by trees, the air was filled with the trill of birdsong, the day fine, and the graves so well tended that no air of melancholy attended the place that marked the demise of the local inhabitants. As they entered the pleasant meadow beyond, they were greeted by the gurgle of a babbling brook. A serpentine path wound its way through this rural idyll and a long range of hills in the distance added a dash of boldness to the picturesque aspect.

"This is quite lovely," said Marianne.

"I thought you would like it." Her aunt smiled. "You have always liked tramping about the countryside. Cheltenham seems to marry the elegancies of town life with the rural in a most unique and pleasing manner. But do follow Lady Georgianna's example and put up your parasol, dear. The sun is already quite warm and you would not wish to acquire freckles."

They had come to a small river; a gently arched wooden bridge led them to a gravel walk, bounded on both sides by rows of tall elm trees. At the end of this noble promenade, an archway gave onto a square court. On one side was the long room, which provided shelter on more inclement days, and on the other, an enclosed area housed an orchestra whose gentle flow of music could not fail to please the ear.

They had barely taken more than a few steps into

the square, when a flamboyantly dressed man, sporting a luridly striped yellow and green waistcoat, which clashed horribly with his blue coat of bath superfine, approached them. His well-cut coat stretched across broad shoulders and framed a figure that was still impressive, if just beginning to thicken a little around the middle. His salt and pepper locks were swept away from a handsome face into which lines of dissipation were clearly marked.

"My dear Fanny," he murmured, bowing low over her hand. "How is it you look even more beautiful in the full glare of day than you do in the muted light of a ballroom?"

Lady Brancaster returned the smile that lurked in his twinkling brown eyes, but said briskly, "What nonsense, Robert. I think age must be dimming your sight or addling your brain. Let me introduce you to my niece, Miss Montagu, and her friend Lady Georgianna Voss. Both of whom can throw me quite into the shade! Girls, this is Sir Robert Pinkington."

He bowed politely to them before offering Lady Brancaster his arm. "Come, allow me to escort you to the pump and procure a glass of the waters for you."

"Oh, very well," she dimpled at him. She glanced over her shoulder. "There are two very nice walks a little further on, my dears, if you would care to explore. I should not be long."

As they walked away, Sir Robert's deep tones drifted back to them.

"Very fine looking gals, Fanny, do you proud, but can't hold a candle to you."

Georgianna raised her expressive brows and Marianne stifled a giggle. She glanced down at Miss Bragg.

"Is Sir Robert the reason Aunt Fanny looks so well? Is he her beau?"

"He is certainly her friend," she said. "He was one of many beaux in her train before she married Lord Brancaster."

"Has he always dressed so colourfully?" Georgianna asked.

"Always. Lady Brancaster told him only the other day that she was not at all sure she wished to be seen with a gentleman who had such an execrable taste in waistcoats."

"I cannot say that I blame her," murmured Georgianna.

Marianne laughed. "You are too severe. Somehow, he carries it off."

"I know exactly what you mean, Miss Montagu," agreed Miss Bragg. "I think it is because he is not at all self conscious about it. He does not care a button what anyone else might think and so it is not worth their time or energy to approve or disapprove his choice of raiment."

"Be that as it may, I think that gentleman looks far more the thing." Georgianna nodded towards the well.

Marianne looked in the general direction she had indicated and then gave her friend a concerned look. "Are you feeling quite all right?" she said, not discerning any trace of humour in her expression. "To be sure he has a fine figure, *I think*, but his shirt points are so high I do not think he can turn his head. And just look at his pantaloons, they are pink, and his coat may be very fine but it is nipped so far in at the waist he must be wearing a corset! Never mind the fact that although he carries a cane, he is limping quite dreadfully!"

"Oh, very droll." Georgianna rolled her eyes in a way her mother would have deplored. "Not him, his companion."

Marianne looked again. This time she noticed the tall, athletic man standing beside him. His clothes were dark and simple. The more eye-catching attire of his friend had at first made him fade into the background, but now she noticed that the cut of his coat was exquisite, his neckcloth tied with neat precision, and the white of his linen almost blinding in the bright sunlight. He had, she thought, a handsome face with regular features and an aquiline nose leading to a firm jaw. His slate grey eyes suddenly swivelled towards her, his expression of weary boredom clear even though fifty yards separated them.

Hurriedly she dropped her eyes, colouring slightly. "Oh, I see. He does look elegant but I think I prefer his friend, he has a smiling, cheerful countenance."

"So does many a fool," Georgianna said dryly.

Miss Bragg gave her a very clear look. "I would not call Sir Horace a fool. That would be unkind, and it is not true. I have had more than one interesting conversation with him in the park in town. But then I know his mother you see and so we have something in common. But I will admit that he is not at his best around young pretty females, he becomes quite tongue-tied or alarmed, and at those moments he is likely to utter the first thing that comes into his head, which is often something quite absurd. It is unfortunate, for you are quite right, Miss Montagu, he is really rather sweet underneath it all."

"And his companion?" Marianne enquired.

Miss Bragg looked thoughtful. "Ah, Lord Cranbourne, I believe, has acquired the reputation of being somewhat dangerous," she said gently. "Although I am not sure it is completely deserved."

"Oh?" said Georgianna. "In what way is he thought to be dangerous?"

Miss Bragg sighed. "Many a matchmaking mama has thrown their daughters in his path, for he is extremely wealthy apart from anything else. But he has raised more than one fair maiden's hope by flirting quite outrageously with them one week, only to seemingly forget all about them the next. This has also earned him the reputation of being heartless and selfish, but I have always thought it a little unfair to *not* expect him to amuse himself with a beautiful – for they are always beautiful – young lady if she is thrown at his head."

Georgianna gave her a rare gentle smile. "You are very magnanimous, Miss Bragg."

"Do you think so?" she said. "I think it is more that I have had the leisure to observe society from the sidelines, particularly before the death of Lord Brancaster, for dear Fanny took me in as a companion long before he died you know, and has always taken me about with her. I have often observed that the young ladies in question used every art to attract him, and I cannot help but think it must become quite tedious to only be sought for your money, especially if you have any degree of intelligence."

"Then it is a shame Lord Wedmore sadly lacks in that department," muttered Georgianna.

"Yes, indeed," murmured Miss Bragg.

"Who are those two ladies over there?" asked Marianne. "They have been staring at us for some moments."

Miss Bragg followed her gaze, smiled, and waved a tentative hand in greeting.

"They are Mrs Frobisher and Mrs Skewitt," she said softly. "They are sisters and have brought their daughters to Cheltenham although I can see no sign of them this morning. They are probably resting after last night's ball for they were both…" she paused as if searching for the right word, "well, very lively. They are probably quite agog to know who you are."

Georgianna raised a haughty brow. "How very rude of them to stare so."

Both ladies were rather stout with keen inquisitive eyes and lips that were rather downturned at the edges. Benevolent persons referred to them as plain, those who were less so, as bracket-faced. They were indeed rather hard faced but then they had suffered the disappointment of witnessing neither of their daughters taking for the last three seasons. Their only small consolation lay in the fact that they had shared the same fate, for neither could have borne to have watched her sister's child succeed where her own had failed.

"Oh dear, they are coming over," Miss Bragg said in a whisper, almost as if she was talking to herself. "I don't suppose they will be pleased, no, not at all."

They did not improve on closer acquaintance. As they were introduced they looked the girls up and down in a very open and appraising way, their eyes narrowing and their lips tightening.

"Lady Georgianna, how very tall you are," Mrs Frobisher said. "It must be such a trial for you."

"Not at all," she replied coolly. "Why should it be?"

Mrs Frobisher's lips spread into a slow smile as if she were forcing long unused muscles into reluctant action. The result was as false as the colour on her brassy hair. "Oh, but gentlemen like their women dainty and feminine do they not? Whereas you must look most of them in the eye!"

"Yes," agreed Georgianna. "I find it very useful, it prevents me from getting a crick in my neck."

Marianne turned her involuntary giggle into a rather unconvincing cough, drawing Mrs Skewitt's attention.

"That is a very pretty parasol, Miss Montagu." She glanced at the pale blue silk appendage, which was once again dangling by Marianne's side rather than sheltering her fair complexion from the sun. "I am surprised your aunt, who always takes such good care of herself, should not have warned you about the danger of freckles, or worse, acquiring a brown skin." She leaned a little nearer and gave her face a close scrutiny. "Oh dear, I think my warning might come too late. I suggest you try Olympian Dew or if that fails, Gowland's Lotion. I am sure Lady Brancaster will have an ample supply."

Marianne obediently snapped her parasol back into place. "Thank you for the advice, Mrs Skewitt," she said with awful politeness. "Tell me, have you found these remedies effective? Or is it perhaps your daughter who has had need of them?"

Both ladies soon took their leave, muttering

various comments about 'modern manners' and 'impertinent misses'.

"A word of advice, girls," said Miss Bragg gently. "Both of those ladies were extremely rude and perhaps deserved a set-down, but not from you. Their lack of breeding does not excuse yours. Cheltenham is a small town and you will make things very uncomfortable for Lady Brancaster if you carry on in that manner."

Marianne and Georgianna both looked a little sheepish.

"However," Miss Bragg continued, "any spiteful remarks that they might make will be put down to jealousy, but only if you show yourselves to have pleasing and modest manners, which in general, you do. You, in particular, Miss Montagu, will not wish to make your come out next season with the reputation of being too coming or impertinent already preceding you. It would be fatal, I assure you."

Her attention was suddenly attracted by a lady who was seated on a bench outside the long room. "Oh, there is Mrs Sandbanks, a dear creature, she is waving so if you will excuse me I will go and pay my respects to her."

"What say we take that walk?" said Marianne, in a subdued tone.

Georgianna took her arm. "Lead on."

They found that the far end of the square gave onto another walk shaded by trees.

"I like Miss Bragg," Georgianna said thoughtfully. "She is very observant and wise, I think. I wonder if she is happy?"

"She has always seemed content."

"Yes, but seeming and being are not always the same thing," murmured Georgianna. "What kind of life can it be to always be on the fringe of society watching others, belonging but not quite belonging?"

"I think she enjoys it," Marianne said after a moment. "Aunt Fanny is very fond of her. She had some sort of connection to her husband. And then, not everyone enjoys being the centre of attention. Or even if they do and make a creditable marriage, it does not ensure that they will be happy."

"No, my own parents are a case in point. Were yours happy?"

"Very." Marianne sighed. "Theirs was a love match."

"Do you think we have a *right* to be happy?" Georgianna mused.

Marianne felt deeply sorry for her friend. It was becoming ever clearer to her that joy had played no great part in her life.

"Yes," she said vehemently. "I do not see why we should not be. Everyone is different of course, and it may be that wealth and consequence are enough to make some people quite content, but my parents were friends and companions too, and if I marry, it is what I would like."

"If?"

"I do not think I am prepared to settle for anything less. And it may be that I shall not find anyone who suits. In which case, I will find another path."

Georgianna wrinkled her brow. "I do not see that you would be left with many options. Do you think you could be happy as a companion like Miss Bragg, or a teacher like Miss Hayes?"

Marianne suddenly giggled. "I do not think I would make a very good teacher."

They turned onto a smaller path that snaked between the trees. It was deliciously cool underneath the boughs although quite gloomy. "Perhaps we should have brought some breadcrumbs!" murmured Marianne.

"The birds would certainly have eaten them." A sardonic grin curled Georgianna's lips. "But at least we are in no danger from any witches, we have left them all behind at the well!"

CHAPTER 5

L ord Cranbourne was not impressed by the pump room. All his worst fears were confirmed. It was full of middle-aged men and ladies quacking themselves with the waters, or mamas who had not managed to attach an eligible bachelor for their plain daughters during the season, and hoped that Cheltenham might offer less competition than Bath and enable them to snabble up the leftovers. He had, admittedly, spotted two very attractive ladies, but if he was not much mistaken they were just out of the schoolroom and he found very young girls a dead bore. He usually found them either tongue-tied, throwing all the burden of conversation upon him, or overly flirtatious, brash even, in their very obvious attempts to please him.

Having dutifully delivered his friend to the well and exchanged a few polite nothings with the odd acquaintance, he decided to take a stroll.

"I will give you half an hour, Bamber," he said. "If

you are not ready by then, you will have to walk back or take a sedan."

He breathed a sigh of relief as he saw the walkway ahead was empty. He could quite see that Cheltenham would suit his friend very well; a bit of congenial company, a good table, and the odd game of billiards if his foot would stand it, or cards if it would not, were all he would require to be content. He, however, would be bored to death before the day was out.

He would never have consented to bring Bamber if the suggestion had not been put to him after a particularly unpleasant interview with his sister. She was a handsome woman, several years older than him. Unfortunately, ever since their mother had died two years earlier, she had seemed to think this seniority gave her the right to take a hand in his affairs. She had summoned him to her house in Grosvenor Street to discover which of his particular friends he would like her to invite down to Cranbourne.

"None of 'em!" he had assured her. "It would look very odd as I have no intention of attending your house party myself."

"You cannot mean it, Anthony," she had protested. "I assure you it was for your benefit that I arranged it."

"If only you had mentioned that to me when you asked if you might invite some friends down to Cranbourne, I would have immediately disabused you of the notion that I wished you to do anything for my benefit, dear sister."

Lady Maria Strickland liked to have her way; if outright bullying and shrill complaint did not achieve her ends, she was not above using more feminine wiles. As she was fully aware that the former tactics could not cow her brother, she resorted to the latter. She had developed the unusual but handy knack of summoning tears at will. She had opened her eyes wide and allowed them to fill, only allowing one or two large drops to spill onto her still smooth cheeks. This usually had the duel benefits of engendering concern or sympathy in her audience whilst ensuring her handsome looks were not rendered hideous. She had dabbed delicately at them with a handkerchief edged in fine lace.

"You are a most unnatural brother. I only wish to see you comfortably settled. It is what dear Mama wished too. Why, when she was in the throes of high fever she grasped my hand and said, 'Dear Maria, keep an eye on your brother when I am gone. I worry for him.'"

Whilst these somewhat underhand tactics usually reduced her husband to putty in her hands, Lord Cranbourne was made of sterner stuff. He had remained distinctly unimpressed.

"That stratagem might work on poor Clifford, but it holds no water with me. There is nothing I detest more than weeping women! Mama must have indeed been out of her senses to have uttered such stuff, if indeed she did! She knew full well that we have no great fondness for each other. It is a piece of high meddling on your part to try and find me a bride. If I had any interest in the Ponsonby girl, or any other female of my acquaintance, I would have already shown it. It is a shame your own girls are too young to make their come out, it would save you disappointment and me irritation if your attentions were directed elsewhere."

He had taken an abrupt leave on these words and retreated to his club. It was there Sir Horace had found him, but not before he had fortified himself with a brandy or two.

Although he had not shown it to his sister, the talk of his mother had unsettled him. He had been close to her. After he had so suddenly and unexpectedly acceded to his father's position, grief at the loss of both him and his brother had swiftly superseded any feelings of betrayal he had felt at Melissa's hands. Although grief-stricken herself, his mother had supported and guided him until the weight of his father's mantle had not weighed so heavily on his shoulders. And although Maria could have no notion of it, they had indeed had a conversation about him choosing a bride before she had suffered the fatal bout of influenza that had forever taken her from him.

"There is no rush," she had assured him gently. "It is just that unless you at least open your mind to the possibility of finding someone who might suit, you are very unlikely to find them."

It had occurred to him that his mother might yearn for some female company and willing to do almost anything to make her happy, he had said, "If you wish me to marry, Mama, I will. Have you anyone in mind?"

Rather than being pleased, she had looked horrified at this dutiful response.

"It would not matter if I did, you must not marry to please me but yourself. Have you met no one for whom you have felt a tendre since Melissa?"

Sitting down beside her he had taken her hands, his eyes softening in the way they did only for her. "You goose, if you think I am still harbouring feelings for Melissa, you are much mistaken!"

"Am I?" she had said softly, her eyes searching his.

"Yes, you are. I have hardly given her a thought for years, and although my memories of that time are painful, it is only because they force me to remember what a cake I made of myself! Whatever gave you the impression that I might still be holding a candle for her?"

"Well, I don't think that precisely," she had said thoughtfully, a frown furrowing her brow. "It is just that…that…" she had trailed off as if not quite certain of what she wished to say.

"It is just what? Come, Mama, you know you can say anything to me."

She had smiled at him in the frank way he loved. "Well, I hope so, my love. It is just that you sometimes seem a little aloof, cold even. Oh, never with me," she had assured him quickly when she had seen his gathering frown. "But when you are in company and even sometimes with your sister."

"Maria is a manipulative baggage," he had said, matching her frankness, his eyes suddenly as hard as granite. "If you wish to talk of being cold, she is a fine example. She cares for nothing but her consequence and comfort. She married Clifford because he could keep her in some style and she would be able to rule him. I do not blame her for that but I do not intend for anyone to be able to rule me!"

"Oh no, of course not, my love," his mother had agreed, raising her hand to cup his cheek. "But be a companion to you, someone to stand beside you and share your burdens and your successes as I have tried to do."

His eyes had softened again and he had turned his head to briefly kiss her hand. "If I could find such a one as you, Mama, I would marry her in an instant, you may be sure!"

A series of short, yappy barks, followed by a lady's scream pulled him from his reverie.

"What the devil?" he said, striding into the trees in the general direction of the commotion.

He paused on the edge of a small circular clearing. On the far side, a diminutive white mongrel, who clearly had a large dose of terrier in his ancestry, stood on his tiny hind legs and was repeatedly leaping to impressive heights in front of one of the huge trees. He was alternately barking and growling at something hidden in the leafy branches above.

One of the two pretty young ladies he had registered earlier was trying to discourage him from his fruitless efforts, the other had backed away and looked concerned for her companion.

"Come away, Marianne," she said sharply. "He will bite you, I am sure of it."

The accused stopped barking for a moment as if offended by the very suggestion and a faint miaow drifted down from above. This seemed to strengthen the resolve of her friend.

"Do not worry, Georgianna," she said. "I think you will find that his bark is worse than his bite!"

As he watched, she lowered her parasol and advanced towards the animal, holding it before her like a shield.

"Shoo, you ridiculous creature," she said in exasperated tones, attempting to gently prod him with the flimsy silk accessory.

The dog looked at her over one shoulder, revealing a narrow face with a circular black patch around one eye. It gave him a disreputable appearance, and living up to his looks he suddenly turned, growled, and obligingly joined in her game – grabbing the parasol with his sharp teeth and tugging it enthusiastically – his sturdy body wriggling in delight and his jauntily curled tail wagging furiously all the time.

The taller of the two ladies shrieked, but her friend remained undaunted. Half laughing, half scolding she said, "Let it go, do, you stupid thing, you will tear it to shreds!"

Lord Cranbourne had seen enough. Although the dog was clearly enjoying himself, he could not be relied upon to maintain his good humour, and if all the young lady suffered was a shredded parasol, she could count herself fortunate. He crossed the grass in three long strides.

"Drop," he said in a confident tone.

Recognising the voice of authority, the dog instantly obeyed, although its small button black eyes never left Marianne and it issued a low warning growl. She took a few steps backwards and the dog followed, still wagging his tail.

"Be still," Lord Cranbourne said. He leaned down swiftly and unhesitatingly grabbed it by the rough ridge of fur at the back of its neck, picked it up and tucked it under his arm.

"That is no way to speak to a lady," he said in stern tones.

The animal turned innocent eyes upon him, his expression clearly indicating that his intentions had been misunderstood, and gave his hand a tentative lick.

"That is all very well," Lord Cranbourne said conversationally. "But you are a disgraceful cur with the manners of a commoner."

The crack of a twig somewhere nearby caught the animal's attention. His ears shot up and he let out another yap, although this one was rather more restrained than those that had gone before. He started to wriggle as a rustic looking gentleman with a rather battered round hat and long smock came upon the scene.

Lord Cranbourne allowed the dog to jump from his arms. He raced over to his master, ran around him in frantic circles a few times, and then sat with his long pink tongue lolling, wagging his tail in rapturous greeting.

The newcomer warily eyed the shredded parasol that hung limply by Marianne's side, its silken shreds gently waving in the light breeze.

"Did he do that, ma'am?" he said with some misgiving.

"He most certainly did," said Georgianna frostily, who not being very well acquainted with the canine family, had been understandably alarmed by recent events. "You should keep that beast of yours locked up!"

"I wouldn't call him a beast, ma'am," the man said, glancing down at the small dog who now sat obediently at his feet as if butter wouldn't melt in his mouth. "And I do keep the gate shut, but that pesky cat appeared out of nowhere and he got to chasing it, which you can hardly blame him for being as it was on his territory like. Dang me if he didn't clear the wall, which must be at least five feet high if it's an inch, in one leap!" he said, not without some pride.

"I suggest you build a higher wall, then," Georgianna snapped.

"Oh, dogs will be dogs," Marianne smiled, completely unconcerned. Her father always had at least three hounds about his heels, although she had never encountered this excitable sort before. "It was my fault really for waving it at him. I should have known better—"

"Yes, you should," drawled Lord Cranbourne in a weary fashion, fastidiously picking dog hairs from his coat. "It would also have been quite your fault if it had bitten you. Over exciting it in that silly way was extremely foolish."

Marianne, who had until that moment been feeling quite grateful to him, looked at him in some astonishment, one eyebrow winging up in challenge.

"Is that so, sir? And were you not inviting the same treatment picking up an unknown dog in that rash manner?"

"No," he stated baldly, "I know dogs."

"So do I," she assured him coolly. "Which is why I have acknowledged already that it was my fault, and so I think it very uncharitable of you to labour the point. But I felt sorry for the cat, she is quite beautiful, you know. She has such glossy night black fur and the most brilliant emerald green eyes. She looks very well cared for and I am sure her owner must be quite concerned. It is my intention to retrieve her and return her."

"Oh?" said Lord Cranbourne, not used to such cavalier treatment but beginning to feel amused anyway. "And how do you mean to achieve the feat? Perhaps you intend to climb the tree?"

His amusement deepened as Marianne craned her neck and looked up thoughtfully, as if seriously considering his suggestion. It was at least fifteen feet to the first branch. "I would certainly need some help. Perhaps you have a ladder, sir?" She turned to the spot where the owner of the errant dog had been standing.

Unfortunately for Marianne, seeing that all attention had been diverted from him to the very fine looking gentleman, he had taken the opportunity to slip quietly away, taking his unruly mutt with him.

"Oh, bother!" said Marianne. "A ladder would have been just the thing!"

"Perhaps," acknowledged Lord Cranbourne, still brushing dog hairs from his sleeve. "And to whom would the honour of climbing it have fallen, I wonder?"

Marianne eyed him with some hostility. "Me, of course. I would not have expected you to do the deed. Heaven forbid that you should risk dirtying your coat even more! And besides, cats can be as dangerous as dogs if they are not handled correctly, and are far more discerning."

Lord Cranbourne's grey eyes began to dance. "Is that so? Am I to deduce then, that if I had put myself to the trouble – which in all honesty I have to admit is unlikely in the extreme – of rescuing the distressed feline, I might have got my eyes scratched out for the trouble?"

Georgianna had been eyeing her friend warily and now bent and whispered something in her ear.

Colouring, Marianne bit her lip. "No, of course not. I must apologise if I seem ungrateful. Thank you for your help, sir, but as the dog has now been removed you may feel free to carry on with whatever it was you were doing before we interrupted you."

Lord Cranbourne was also unused to being so summarily dismissed, but he bowed politely and retreated from the glade, surprised to register a slight feeling of disappointment. Whatever else the unexpected encounter had been, it had certainly not been boring.

"What a rude, disagreeable man," Marianne muttered as soon as he was out of earshot. "It is just as well you reminded me of Miss Bragg's warning or I might have said something outrageous!"

"You already had! What is more, I did not think him disagreeable. He dealt with the situation in a very expeditious and effective manner. I dread to think what might have happened if he had not come to our rescue."

"Come to our rescue? It was no such thing and I will tell you precisely what would have happened. That dear little dog would have become bored presently and gone after less elusive prey. Have you no dogs at your home?"

"No, thank goodness. They make Mama sneeze."

"Oh, then I quite see why you were so afraid. It is a shame, for I assure you they are generally very affectionate creatures, make excellent guard dogs, and are frequently most amusing."

"I was not afraid," Georgianna said haughtily. "I am never afraid. I admit I was a little apprehensive on your account, however."

Feeling a trifle disappointed that her friend had not entered into her feelings about Lord Cranbourne, she said softly, "Never afraid? Not even of marrying Lord Wedmore?"

"Certainly not. I do not know why I said that. It would be more accurate to say that I feel repelled by the prospect."

Never one to stay annoyed for long, Marianne sighed and smiled ruefully. "I am sorry, that was unkind of me. I do not know why I let Lord Cranbourne put me in such a pelter."

Georgianna accepted the olive branch. "Perhaps he was a little overbearing."

Marianne laughed. "Well, I do think it the outside of enough when a complete stranger calls you silly and foolish!"

Another miaow issued from the tree. Seeing the coast was clear, the harried feline scrambled down the trunk a few feet, and then leaped gracefully through the air, landing neatly on the grass.

Marianne knelt down and put out her hand. "Here, puss," she murmured softly.

Recognising a friend, the cat padded over to her and rubbed its head against her palm. She picked it up gently and Georgianna gave it a tentative stroke.

"She is quite lovely," she acknowledged. "Very aristocratic. But how will you find out who owns her?"

They began to walk back towards the pump room. "I am sure the owner will put up a notice in one of the shops or libraries," Marianne said confidently. "If they do not, I will."

CHAPTER 6

When Marianne returned to the pump room with a ruined parasol, grass stains on her dress, and a cat in her arms, Lady Brancaster began to realise that she might have taken on more than she had bargained for. Without waiting for explanations, she hastily bundled her niece into a sedan chair before she could excite unwanted comment or speculation, with instructions for her to be returned to St George's Place with all possible haste.

It fell to Lady Georgianna to describe what had occurred as they walked back to the house.

"I see," Lady Brancaster said faintly when she had come to the conclusion of her tale. "How very intrepid Marianne is, to be sure. I suppose I should be grateful I have not acquired a vicious dog into the bargain."

"Do not be angry with her, ma'am," Lady Georgianna said, as she saw a frown pucker her brows. "Marianne has a very kind heart; she did not wish the owner to worry any longer than need be. I have every reason to be grateful for that kindness for without it I would still be languishing at Miss Wolfraston's seminary. She invited me to accompany her here before we had even become friends." A faint flush gave colour to her naturally pale complexion. "In truth, I had not been a pleasant companion and had spurned any attempts at friendliness towards me."

Lady Brancaster smiled at her distractedly. "I don't suppose you knew any better, dear. And I am not angry, but although I am glad some of Marianne's openness of manner has rubbed off on you, I could wish that some of your reserve had rubbed off on her!"

Georgianna smiled. "Miss Wolfraston said something very similar before we left."

"I blame her father," Lady Brancaster continued. "And myself a little. I should have paid more attention after her mother died but I was quite cut up about it all myself, and then my poor Samuel followed her to the Lord. I think Marianne became her father's companion in her stead, which is all very well, but it has not helped her learn how to comport herself as a lady should. And Miss Wolfraston's seminary has obviously done nothing at all to alter the case."

"I think her naturalness of manner is quite charming," Miss Bragg said.

Lady Brancaster suddenly came to a standstill and gave Georgianna an intent look. "Although I can quite see that I have every reason to be thankful for Lord Cranbourne's timely intervention, I would not have wished you to meet him unchaperoned. Tell me, did he find her charming, do you think?"

"I doubt it, ma'am. One of the things I admire about Marianne is that although she is kind, she is not at all milky. She is never afraid to challenge someone if she thinks they are being unjust. I know that to my cost!"

Lady Brancaster groaned. "Do not tell me she has put his back up! It would only take a few wicked words from him when she makes her come out and her season will be ruined!"

"She did not say anything too outrageous, ma'am, I assure you."

"Do not fret yourself to flinders, Fanny," Miss Bragg advised. "From what I have observed, Lord Cranbourne is a restless creature. I doubt very much that he will remain here very long. Indeed, I cannot imagine what induced him to come in the first place for he cannot need to take the waters, and as pleasant as Cheltenham is, it is not exactly in the first stare of fashion. But one thing I am sure of is that he will have forgotten all about the incident within a sennight."

When there was no sign of Lord Cranbourne over the next two days, Lady Brancaster began to relax. It seemed that Miss Bragg had been correct in her prediction that he would not kick his heels in Cheltenham for long. And as Marianne was on her best behaviour and had given her no further reason to worry about her conduct, she looked forward to escorting her young guests to their very first ball. These occurred every Monday and Friday in the summer season, their location alternating between the upper and lower rooms.

Unlike Lady Westbury, she would enjoy introducing two such very lovely girls to her acquaintances, and although she was not generally vindictive, the prospect had the added spice of knowing how much that lady would dislike it. Serena Saddlingham as she had been then, had always been a spiteful little cat and had disliked Fanny on sight. That her starched up manners had led more than one of her admirers to defect to her light-hearted rival, had set the seal on her hatred.

Although Fanny had always enjoyed the attention her own good looks and good taste had brought her, she was not obsessed by them and certainly not foolish enough to think herself in competition with her two beautiful young guests.

She had surprised many when she had accepted Lord Brancaster's offer over all the others she had received, some from very dashing blades, but she had been very happy in her marriage in the end. Whilst not being overly given to introspection, she knew she was not of a strong disposition and had recognised qualities in Lord Brancaster that she lacked herself.

Her husband had been much older than her and had been considered a confirmed bachelor by the *ton*. He was by nature serious but he had adored her unconditionally. He had seemed to know instinctively how to handle his flighty bride, treating her gently but firmly, and for her part, she had always been able to draw him out and make him laugh. Lady Brancaster had come to love him, not in a mad passionate way, but with a deep and lasting regard and she had genuinely mourned his passing.

Her only lasting regret was that she had never managed to present him with a child, something he had never berated her for, but on the contrary, had informed her with the unerring logic that was typical of him, that as he had never considered the wedded state until he had made her acquaintance, it could not signify.

She was determined however, to stand in the place of a mother to Marianne during her stay. When she had invited her to bring a friend to Cheltenham, she had vaguely thought that she could allow them to meander about the place on their own, with a maid in tow, of course. She had revised that idea on seeing the pair of them together, realising that they were bound to attract no small degree of attention, and she had hardly let them out of her sight since the incident at the pump room.

When she entered her bedchamber on the night of the ball, the sight that met her brought tears to her eyes. She had made a present of Marianne's first ball gown, designing it herself and having it made up by a most superior seamstress. The results were breathtaking.

"What do you think?" Marianne laughed, "Will I do?"

The dress was deceptively simple, with a white crape petticoat over white satin, but it was embroidered in silver lama at the base, the trim repeated below the modest bosom. It twinkled in the candle-light as Marianne twirled gracefully to display it from all angles.

"You look beautiful, my child," Lady Brancaster sighed. "I only wish your mother could see you! She would be so proud."

Marianne's expression sobered and she rushed

forward to embrace her aunt. "Thank you, Aunt Fanny," she said softly.

Lady Brancaster briefly returned the embrace before stepping away. "Enough. I will never forgive you if you make me cry; it always makes the tip of my nose horribly red. Besides, Nancy has made such a fine job of your hair, and you will quite ruin it if you don't stop flouncing about."

Marianne cast a quick look in her mirror, turning her head this way and that to check all was still in order. Her dark locks fell in irregular curls at the front, falling low on each side of her face. A bandeau decorated with pearls was twisted around others that clustered behind her head.

"You are right. Nancy took an age and would certainly rake me down if she had to start again."

The door opened as she spoke and Georgianna stepped into the room. Her mother might not have wished her to attend any balls, but neither could she bear for it to be said that any daughter of hers was a dowd. Consequently, she had sent Georgianna all that she might require. Knowing her complexion to be almost preternaturally pale, she did not make the mistake of decking her out only in white. She wore a white satin slip under a dress of gros de Naples, but folds of satin in mazarine blue and white were alternately layered, and a border of white roses decorated the hem. Her hair was drawn smoothly on the crown of her head and then twisted high into a neat knot, its only ornament, a single white rose set against her ebony locks.

"Very striking," Lady Brancaster approved. "The

blue stripes almost exactly match your eyes. My compliments to your mother."

Her gaze returned to her niece and rested pensively there for a moment. "I hope you won't mind me saying this Marianne. I do not mean to be forever scolding you – it makes me feel quite ancient apart from anything else – but please ensure the elegance of your manners match the elegance of your dress, whether you are provoked or not!"

Far from taking umbrage, Marianne's eyes twinkled with amusement. "Of course, Aunt. I would not repay your generosity and kindness by behaving badly. Although I never mean to, you know. I suppose you were a pattern card of respectability when you made your come out?"

Lady Brancaster grimaced. "No, but I was very fortunate to marry Lord Brancaster before I could quite sink myself beneath reproach! There is no one who knows better than I how easy it is for liveliness to carry one too far."

"Really?" said Marianne, intrigued. "Do I smell a scandal?"

Lady Brancaster raised her fine eyebrows and gave her niece a stern look. "Certainly not. Now come along, or we will be horribly late."

Lord Cranbourne had not yet deserted his friend. He had been venting some of his excess energy by hiring a hack and discovering the many scenic rides which littered this part of the country, generally returning mud splattered and tired just in time to dine with Sir Horace.

On the day of the ball, discovering the horse he had been given was a veritable slug, he returned earlier than usual. He took a stroll along High Street and was enticed into Mrs Jones's circulating library by the wide selection of newspapers on offer.

He was idly perusing the advertisements in the Morning Post when he heard himself addressed.

"Mind if I take a seat, Cranbourne?"

He glanced up and allowed his eyes to feast upon Sir Robert Pinkington's luxurious red and gold waistcoat for a moment. He had been surprised when he had spotted him in the pump room. Although he dressed like a dandy, he knew full well that he was a sporting gentleman who was a bruising rider and very handy with his fives. Being some years older than himself, he was not closely acquainted with him, although their paths had crossed now and again as they were both members of the four-horse club. He would not have thought this small spa town had anything much to offer him.

"Feel free, Sir Robert," he said with a small smile. "The paper is so dull today I have been reduced to looking at the advertisements. Would you believe that there is a lady, highly respectable she assures us, who possesses property, is agreeable in both person and manners, and would be happy to form an alliance with a gentlemen who shares these attributes as a friend and companion through life?"

Sir Robert grimaced. "Advertising for a husband? If she is forced to find a companion for life in such a manner, she must be desperate. She is most likely ugly as sin. Perhaps we should inform Brummel of this lady; rumour has it he is in desperate straits. I'm sure her 'property' would keep him out of dun territory for at least a month! What is the address?"

Lord Cranbourne glanced again at the advertisement. "Tottenham Court Road."

"Then I fear she must forgo him as a companion, that location would never do for our fastidious friend."

Lord Cranbourne knew that there was no love lost between the two. Rumour had it that Sir Robert had stubbornly stuck to his flamboyant way of dressing in direct response to Brummel becoming the so-called arbiter of fashion.

"And then," he added, "one could never call him agreeable. Indeed, now that his cutting tongue has irrevocably lost him the friendship and goodwill of Prinny, I hear his creditors are descending on him in droves!"

Although he himself adopted the more restrained mode of dressing favoured by Brummel, Lord Cranbourne really had very little interest in the man himself. And knowing from painful experience that people who were allowed to run on about their pet hates invariably became dead bores, he turned the subject. "I am surprised to find you here. Do not tell me you have come to take the waters?"

"Very well," he replied. "I will not. I assume that you also have not been tempted to imbibe them?"

Lord Cranbourne grinned. "I should hope not, they smell foul. However, if they had a reputation for curing addled brains, I might be tempted. I agreed to bring Bamber down in a fit of madness and have been regretting it ever since!"

Sir Robert gave him a sympathetic smile. "It has always amazed me that the two of you are such firm friends. I have nothing at all to say against Sir Horace, I'm sure, but his understanding has never struck me as anything more than moderate."

"No," agreed Lord Cranbourne. "But our lands march together and so I have known him forever. He used to follow me around like a faithful hound when we were children. I will say this for him; he was always game for a lark. When we were sent to school he was bullied a trifle and I looked out for him. It has become a hard habit to break."

Sir Robert's rather aloof gaze warmed a touch. "He is fortunate to have such a loyal friend."

Lord Cranbourne shrugged carelessly. "I do not know about that, but upsetting Bamber would be like kicking a puppy. I do not think you mentioned what had brought you to this dreadfully dull place, care to enlighten me?"

Sir Robert leant back in his chair and looked thoughtfully at his companion. "I am not at all sure that I do," he said softly. "It is a rather delicate matter."

Lord Cranbourne read into these words the implication that he was not to be trusted and rose swiftly to his feet. "In that case, I will take my leave of you."

"Oh, do not be so testy, Cranbourne," Sir Robert said frowning. "Sit down, please. I meant no offence. The trouble is I see in you far too much of myself when I was a young man.

As Sir Robert had acquired the reputation of being something of a rake over the years, Lord Cranbourne's brows winged upwards. Intrigued, he sat down again.

"This concerns a lady, I take it."

"Indeed it does, dear chap. That elusive creature that one never quite forgets – the one that got away!"

Lord Cranbourne began to look amused. "Ah, I see. You have followed her to Cheltenham and hope to finally catch her in your toils. I wish you luck, but where do I come in? I do not wish to sound like a coxcomb, but are you afraid I will cut you out?"

Sir Robert gave a bark of laughter. "No, I am not afraid of that. The lady concerned has, I believe, a fondness for me."

"Do I know her?"

"I should think so, although she has been living quite retired from society for the last few years, mourning her husband. It is Lady Brancaster."

"A widow! Well then, if she has a fondness for you I can see no difficulty in you enjoying an affaire de coeur for the summer. It must be at least three years since Lord Brancaster went to meet his maker. I do not know the lady well, but I seem to recall that apart from being very easy on the eye, she was extremely engaging. Always seemed to have a host of admirers gathered about her."

Sir Robert's brows snapped together in a frown. "Perhaps I should inform you that surprising as it may seem, my intentions towards this lady are strictly honourable. And although you are correct in your observation that she has always been very popular, she has always behaved with honour and integrity, I assure you."

Lord Cranbourne's brows arched upwards. "Very

well. I did not mean to cast aspersions on Lady Brancaster's character. And although I am, of course, honoured by your confidences, I am still unclear as to why you are sharing them with me."

Sir Robert's brow cleared, he leaned forwards and spoke in hushed tones. "I am hoping that you might offer me your aid. Lady Brancaster has invited a couple of girls just out of the schoolroom to stay with her. She is taking her role as chaperone very seriously and it is cramping my style somewhat. I was hoping it might offer you some amusement to, let us say, develop an acquaintance with them. They are both very striking after all."

A small smile curved Lord Cranbourne's lips. "Although I have not been formally introduced, I have a feeling I may have come across them already."

"I am aware. It is why I thought of you. Come to the ball at the upper rooms tonight and get to know them better."

Lord Cranbourne looked a touch rueful. "As you say, Sir Robert, there are some similarities between us. Although my past is not perhaps as chequered as yours, it may be that Lady Brancaster may not welcome any overtures of friendship I might make. And, even putting that hurdle aside, I think you will find that one of them, at least, thinks me a paltry sort of fellow."

Sir Robert was not to be put off. His whole demeanour suddenly resonated with purpose. "Lady Brancaster already feels herself to be in your debt, I believe. Lady Georgianna, that is the tall, proud one, seems to have persuaded her that you rescued Miss Montagu from being mauled by an extraordinarily vicious animal. As for the girls themselves, I do not believe for an instant that someone of your experience and address could not bring both of them around your finger if you so wished."

When Lord Cranbourne still looked undecided, he added earnestly, "If you must have it, I wish Lady Brancaster to be my wife. But persuading her I have changed will not be an easy task and it will be an impossible one if I cannot ensure I have her undivided attention at least some of the time!"

"I see," Lord Cranbourne said seriously. The sudden intensity of his companion's manner left him in no doubt of his sincerity. That Lady Brancaster had captured his heart could not be in doubt.

The image of the girl with chocolate brown eyes, a snub nose, and an arch manner, whom he now knew to be Miss Montagu, swam into Lord Cranbourne's mind. She really had been very pretty. It had been refreshing to meet a young lady who had seemed to have no interest in impressing him. He gave a soft chuckle. On the contrary, she had not hesitated to spar with him. He had promised Bamber he would stay a week at least, that left him a few more days of tedium to endure. He supposed it might be amusing to see if he could win her approval. He only hoped it would take that long or she would become as tiresome as any other young lady of his acquaintance, he was sure.

"I will play your game," he said, at last. "But I warn you now, you will have only a little time to work your magic. I will be gone by the end of this week, at the very latest."

Sir Robert smiled and shook his hand to seal the deal. "You are the best of good fellows, Cranbourne. I will suggest to Fanny that we all go on an outing tomorrow. Bring Sir Horace to even up the numbers a trifle. Not even the most concerned chaperone has any worries about Sir Horace."

Lord Cranbourne suddenly laughed. "They will terrify him!"

"One thing, Cranbourne. I do not wish you to compromise the ladies in any way, it would reflect badly on Lady Brancaster and not help my cause at all."

Sir Robert suddenly found himself on the receiving end of what Sir Horace called his baleful glare.

"I am not in the habit of seducing young ladies of quality."

"Climb down from your high ropes, Cranbourne. I did not really think that you were, just making the rules of the game clear."

CHAPTER 7

Marianne was surprised that they were to take a carriage to the ball, as it was only a very short walk from St George's Place.

"That is beside the point, my dear." Lady Brancaster sighed. "It will not do for you to turn up with dust on your slippers, neither would it add to your consequence if you were to arrive in such a commonplace way."

The upper assembly rooms were spacious and airy. They were very well lit by a series of elegant glass chandeliers suspended from the ceiling. The ball started promptly at eight o'clock and as they arrived with only ten minutes to spare, it was already filled with a great number of people and buzzed with the hum of quiet conversation.

Mr King, the master of ceremonies, wasted no time in acknowledging their presence. Although of quite an advanced age, he had a pleasing, benevolent countenance and a sprightly demeanour.

"So your guests have arrived, Lady Brancaster.

May I say that it can only add to the success of our modest assembly to have such elegant persons as yourselves attend it?"

His words, although deferential in character, were stripped of any hint of obsequiousness by the natural charm of his manner.

"It is too kind of you to say so," Lady Brancaster said graciously.

"You may be assured that I shall make sure both Lady Georgianna and Miss Montagu are never without a partner, should they wish for one. Ah, I see Sir Robert is approaching and so I will take my leave." He bowed and moved on to another group.

Marianne noticed a faint colour stain her aunt's cheeks as she quickly glanced up. She followed her gaze and smiled. There was nothing garish about Sir Robert's dress this evening. He wore a corbeau coloured coat, a white marcella waistcoat, and black breeches of Florentine silk. Even her untrained eye could tell he looked quite splendid.

"He looks very smart, doesn't he?" Georgianna whispered in her ear.

"Yes, Aunt Fanny is very pleased, I think."

"Oh, Sir Robert's attire is a vast improvement, but I was referring to Lord Cranbourne."

In the press of people, Marianne had not noticed the man walking in Sir Robert's wake, but as they drew closer the crowd cleared a little and he resumed his position beside him.

"I might have known they would be friends," muttered Lady Brancaster underneath her breath. "Peas out of the same pod!"

Marianne barely heard her. If Sir Robert looked

splendid, then she had to reluctantly acknowledge that Lord Cranbourne looked quite magnificent. They were of a similar height and build, but the younger man's hair was raven black and his face unlined. He moved with athletic grace and oozed restrained vitality. His white silk stockings displayed muscled, finely-shaped calves and his close fitting coat accentuated his trim waist and broad shoulders.

She gave herself a mental shake. He might look impressive, but she doubted very much if he cared for much more than the cut of his coat! He may have come to her rescue but he had been more concerned with the hairs on his sleeve than any shock she might have received. That she had not suffered from any such shock was neither here nor there, he had not known that when he had called her silly and foolish!

After the formal introductions were made, Sir Robert bowed low over Lady Brancaster's hand. "I have been counting the hours, oh cruel one."

She rapped him lightly on the arm with her fan. "What nonsense, Robert, I saw you only yesterday."

"That is why I say you are cruel. I waited in vain for you to come to the well this morning. Despite the water, it was a desert without you. I have rarely been more disappointed."

Lady Brancaster's colour deepened to a delightful shade of pink. "Stop spouting such flummery. You know I have guests who have more claim on my time than you, Robert."

She turned to Lord Cranbourne. "I am glad to see you, sir, for I have not yet had the opportunity to thank you for dealing so promptly with that nasty little dog. Lady Georgianna assures me that your intervention was most timely."

He gave Lady Brancaster a respectful bow. "It was my honour to offer my services to both Lady Georgianna and Miss Montagu."

Marianne was fully alive to the satirical glance he sent in her direction as he spoke her name. Despite meaning to be on her best behaviour, she raised her chin a fraction and smiled sweetly at him. "Have you managed to remove all the dog hairs from your coat, sir?"

His gaze narrowed. "No, but my assiduous valet has achieved the difficult and no doubt tedious feat," he drawled.

His languid air was slightly too exaggerated. No fool, Marianne began to realise that she was being baited.

The steady tap of a cane against the polished wooden floor caught her attention. The man Miss Bragg had called Sir Horace was making his awkward way towards them.

"I say, old chaps, it really is the outside of enough that you drag me here and then abandon me in so callous a manner to, to, what was her name now? Skewer? Skeweth? No, that's not right. Skewitt! Mrs Skewitt and her abominable d—"

He broke off hurriedly as Lord Cranbourne turned and revealed they were in company. Casting a rather alarmed gaze over Marianne and Georgianna, he sent a look of unconscious appeal in the direction of Miss Bragg.

Stepping forwards she smiled kindly at him.

"Good evening, Sir Horace. How wonderful to see you again after all this time."

Her gentle tones seemed to do the trick, his expression turned from startled to wary.

"Yes, I must agree. How is your dear mother?" added Lady Brancaster.

Put at his ease by these two good ladies, he even managed a creditable bow to the younger members of the party.

The first dance was announced and Lord Cranbourne turned to Marianne.

"May I have the pleasure of this dance, Miss Montagu?"

She glanced at her aunt and received an affirmative nod.

As Mr King appeared with a partner for Georgianna and Sir Robert claimed Lady Brancaster, she accepted graciously, laid her hand lightly on his arm, and allowed him to lead her to the long line of dancers just forming.

The honour of calling the dance fell to Lady Brancaster and Sir Robert. Marianne watched very carefully for a few moments and felt a mixture of pride and pleasure as she watched her aunt's neatly executed steps. She was pleased to hear she had chosen a moderate tempo; although she enjoyed a lively romp as much as the next person, for reasons not entirely clear to her, she found she did not wish to appear any less elegant than her partner.

Once they had settled into the rhythm of the dance, she found she was enjoying herself so much she momentarily forgot that she did not like her partner.

Involuntarily, she gave him an unconsciously warm smile.

"This is far better than dance practice," she said confidingly.

Lord Cranbourne's lips quirked and one dark brow winged up. "Am I to take it that this is your first ball, Miss Montagu? I would never have guessed. You dance very well."

"So do you, sir."

His eyes glimmered with amusement. "I am honoured by your compliment, Miss Montagu, but your achievement must outweigh mine for I have had a vast amount of experience."

"Yes, so I have heard."

She winced as the figure of the dance took her away from him for a moment. Blast her wretched tongue. She had spoken without thinking, it was her besetting sin. As her new partner spun her around her eyes briefly met her aunt's. She pinned what she hoped was a reassuring smile on her lips.

When she returned to her place opposite her partner, she glanced cautiously up at him, her cheeks still warm with embarrassment.

"I apologise, my lord, if I spoke out of turn."

"Oh, please do not put on your society manners, Miss Montagu. I find it refreshing to not be able to predict what you will say next."

"I am beginning to realise it is a serious failing." She looked a little downcast. "My father used to laugh at the things I said, but I can quite see that it will not do if I am to make a creditable appearance in society. But old habits are so hard to break aren't they?"

Lord Cranbourne looked at her very intently for a moment, and then gave her a rueful smile. "Very." He swiftly turned the subject. "Tell me, Miss Montagu, have you managed to return the cat you rescued to its owner? I saw you had placed a notice in Mrs Jones's window."

Her brow wrinkled. "No. I do not understand it, but no one has come to claim her. It is a pity for Aunt Fanny is not fond of cats. She has banished her to the kitchen, which is a shame, for I feel sure she was a pet and not a mouser."

"Just out of interest, how did you rescue her?"

"I did not need to. She rescued herself once the dog had gone."

"Ah, I see. Well might I suggest, Miss Montagu, that if you let the cat out, it might find its own way home? They have a reasonable sense of direction, I believe."

Marianne looked at him thoughtfully. "You may be right."

"I usually am," he murmured.

Marianne's eyes flashed with annoyance for a brief moment but then she gave a small gurgle of laughter.

"If I am not much mistaken, you are trying to provoke me. Why?"

"Your eyes sparkle beautifully when you are angry," he said smoothly.

The movement of the dance parted them again. When they came together again, she gave him a considering look.

"I *think* you are flirting with me."

"Not very well if you only *think* it," he said dryly.

"Well, I have had no experience yet, so I should not perhaps comment on your proficiency in the art."

He quirked an ironic brow. "Something tells me that you will anyway."

She gurgled again. "Well, I must admit, it did not seem a very original thing to say."

The music came to an end and he escorted her from the floor.

"Perhaps you will do me the honour of dancing with me again later, Miss Montagu, so I can, er, tune up my technique."

"Certainly," she agreed as he delivered her to Miss Bragg. "I will enjoy the practice."

She looked down at Sir Horace. "How is your foot, sir? It is such a pity that you cannot dance."

He looked amazed at her perspicacity. "That's the problem in a nutshell, Miss Montagu. Can't dance. Make a hash of it every time. Blow me if I can remember the steps and I always end up standing on someone's toes or confusing everybody. It becomes a dashed awkward business, I can tell you."

Marianne's eyes danced. She found Mr King at her elbow but shook her head.

"I think I will sit this one out, I wish to talk to Sir Horace."

His brows shot up and he turned an interesting shade of red. "I say, Miss Montagu, that's dashed kind of you, but I would not wish to deprive you of a dance."

"Don't give it a thought, Sir Horace. The evening is yet young and there will be plenty more, after all."

The rest of the party came up and Lord Cranbourne intercepted a meaningful look from Sir Robert. He would very much like to have heard the conversation between Miss Montagu and Bamber, but dutifully invited Lady Georgianna to dance.

He found her very much more reserved than her friend and was glad that the lively cotillion left little opportunity for conversation. She was graceful and very beautiful, but he thought her face lacked the animation of Miss Montagu. He performed the steps of the dance automatically and his inherent good manners ensured that none of the dancers guessed that his thoughts were elsewhere.

Several of Miss Montagu's comments had been outrageous, but they were delivered with such an engaging frankness that it was impossible to take offence. At least he had found that to be the case. She was neither a coquette nor a simpering miss. On the contrary, she was charming and unaffected. He would have to wait until much later to invite her to dance again if he did not wish to invite comment and he was surprised to discover that this irked him.

Once he had finished his turn with Lady Georgianna, he whisked Sir Horace off to the card room.

"I say, old chap, Miss Montagu is really quite delightful. Not like your usual gal on the lookout for a husband."

Lord Cranbourne glanced down at him thoughtfully. "I do not think Miss Montagu has given that consideration any thought at all."

"Do you know, I think you might be right? Well all I can say is, it is downright refreshing."

"Not taken a fancy for her yourself, have you, Bamber?"

"Now hold on a minute, Cranbourne, can't a

fellow express admiration for a female without his friends casting aspersions on him?"

"I think you are a trifle confused, Bamber. I am not suggesting you have any nefarious intentions, merely asking if she might tempt you to abandon your single state."

"Oh, I see. Sorry Cranbourne, thought it meant something quite different. That's the problem with the English language, ain't it? So many words to choose from, it's hardly surprising one occasionally gets befuddled. The short answer is no."

Lord Cranbourne's grey eyes turned to silver and his lips quivered with suppressed amusement. "Dare I ask what the long answer is?"

"I see what it is. You are roasting me. You know full well that I wouldn't know what to do with a female. Most of 'em scare me to death. Miss Montagu don't. She has no airs or graces and I like her the better for it. First young female that hasn't made me feel like an idiot. You know exactly where you are with her, if you know what I mean."

Lord Cranbourne gave his friend a lopsided smile. "For once, Bamber, your meaning is crystal clear. I know exactly what you mean."

It wasn't until the tea break that he encountered her again. Sir Robert, keeping a weather eye out, spotted them the moment they entered the room and invited them to join his party. Lord Cranbourne moved towards a chair that was free next to Miss Montagu, but despite his limp, Sir Horace was before him.

If he had wished she might experience some slight

disappointment at this event, the warm welcome with which she greeted his friend soon dispelled it as a forlorn hope. Without missing a beat, he pulled out the chair for Sir Horace as if that had been his intention all along. He then strolled casually around the other side of the table and took the place next to Lady Georgianna, who was sat so rigidly upright, he could almost imagine she had a stick wedged down the back of her dress.

"That was very well done, Lord Cranbourne." Her lips curved in a satirical smile. "I could almost believe you had wished to sit beside me."

"I can assure you it is my pleasure to have the opportunity to converse with you, Lady Georgianna. I believe Sir Robert mentioned that you and Miss Montagu attended the same seminary?"

Georgianna inclined her head regally. "That is correct."

"You must give me the direction. I shall write to whoever runs it and compliment her on running such a forward thinking establishment."

"But it is not any such thing. Whatever gave you that idea?"

"The forthright and unusual conversation of its pupils," he said dryly.

Georgianna's lips twitched. "Ah, but as Miss Montagu and myself only attended for two terms, I hardly think you can lay our merits or our failings at Miss Wolfraston's door. Our friend, Charlotte, attended for much longer than us, and she was all that is meek and mild, I assure you."

"I am relieved to hear it."

Georgianna raised a haughty brow. "Because that is the sort of female you approve of?"

"No. Because it will save me the trouble of writing that letter."

Georgianna was surprised into a smile.

"That is better," Lord Cranbourne said. "I was beginning to feel distinctly chilly."

Lady Brancaster had been standing a short distance away in close conversation with Sir Robert, but she now approached her charges.

"Would you like to drive out into the countryside tomorrow, girls? Sir Robert has suggested we take a blanket and enjoy an al fresco nuncheon."

This suggestion was greeted with universal approval.

"There are many pretty spots around here," Lord Cranbourne confirmed. "As I have already explored many of them, might I suggest you allow me to be your guide?"

"What a splendid idea, Cranbourne," Sir Robert instantly approved. "I would have had to rely upon a guidebook, but they so often prove disappointingly inaccurate, don't they?"

"Do they?" Lady Brancaster said, clearly a little put out.

"Oh yes, my dear," Sir Robert assured her. "They are so often written by local people who naturally think their little patch of England vastly superior to any other. They cannot be objective in their descriptions. Their idea of a spectacular view not to be matched anywhere else in the country, to an outsider is no such thing. Much better to rely on a visitor who has formed a pleasing impression of a place."

"And so much less trouble for you, Robert."

He gave her a very direct look and said with gentle

sincerity, "You are mistaken, Fanny. No service I could render you would be too much trouble."

"Do say you will come too, Sir Horace," Marianne said, breaking the tension that seemed to arc between her aunt and Sir Robert.

"Be delighted," he beamed. "Do you know, I don't think these waters are all they are cracked up to be? Didn't go this morning and I feel the better for it. Won't do any harm to miss them tomorrow. And don't you worry about the food, Lady Brancaster. It will be my pleasure to bring it."

She smiled at him. "Thank you, Sir Horace. It seems I am left with very little to do."

In an attempt to soothe Lady Brancaster's ruffled feathers, Lord Cranbourne claimed her hand for the next dance.

"I take it you are here to keep Sir Horace company, Lord Cranbourne?" she enquired as they took to the floor.

"You are correct, ma'am, but only for a few days longer."

He thought she looked relieved.

"I did not mean to appear ungrateful earlier, Lord Cranbourne. It is very generous of you to give up your time to be our guide."

He grinned engagingly at her. "I completely understand, ma'am. But let us not beat around the bush. You are concerned that I might not be the ideal company for your two young charges. To put not too fine a point upon it, you wonder what my intentions might be."

Lady Brancaster had always had a soft corner for a charming rake. Her dimples peeped as she returned his smile. "It is so much easier isn't it, to cut right to the chase rather than wrap everything up in clean linen? You are right, of course."

Her eyes sparkled with an imp of mischief as she gave him a knowing look. Although their colouring was quite different, something indefinable about her reminded him of her niece.

"I may have been living a little retired in recent times, but that does not mean I do not hear all the latest on dits."

"And what is it that you have heard?" he asked a little warily.

"That you can flirt outrageously with a girl one moment, and just when her hopes are raised, forget all about her the next!"

He smiled ruefully down at her. "I may sometimes have punished a young lady in just such a fashion, but only if they deserved it, I assure you. I do not think you need worry about Miss Montagu; she has already informed me that my flirting is woefully unoriginal. I have promised to try to improve it and she is looking forwards to the exercise."

Lady Brancaster gasped and then gave a trill of laughter. "Well, that put you in your place. It is all innocence you know, there is nothing contrived about Marianne."

"I am aware of that, ma'am. Suffice it to say that my intentions are merely to relieve the tedium of the next few days, nothing more. Neither of the young ladies are in any danger from me. If anything, the boot is on the other foot."

"Oh, in what way?"

"I fear exposure to them for any length of time might reduce my confidence to the level of Bamber's."

Lady Brancaster laughed. "Poor Sir Horace. He is a dear. It is such a pity he is such a nodcock around the ladies. There is nothing Lady Bamber would like more than to see him settled."

"Then I fear she is doomed to disappointment. He has taken a rare liking to Miss Montagu, admittedly, but only because she doesn't scare him half to death."

Lady Brancaster looked a little troubled. "You don't think…?"

"No, ma'am," Lord Cranbourne interrupted her. "You need have no worries on that head. I have been assured that he has no intention of entering the married state."

As the dance came to an end, a piercing scream rent the air. For a brief moment, time seemed suspended as all occupants of the room froze; almost as if a spell had been cast upon them, their startled eyes fixed on a spot in the middle of the floor.

A portly gentleman had collapsed at the feet of his partner. Unfortunately he had been violently sick all over her slippers. A cacophony of shrill voices shattered the silence as horrified onlookers gathered their wits and scattered to the edges of the room.

Lord Cranbourne swiftly delivered Lady Brancaster to Miss Bragg, who was standing quietly with Sir Horace.

"Never seen anything like it," Sir Horace spluttered. "At least, not at a public assembly! Don't understand it. He can't be intoxicated, they only serve that insipid tea here."

"Never mind that, Bamber, see the ladies get home

safely. Sir Robert and I will see if we can be of any use."

Their help proved to be superfluous. Mr King acted with decision and efficiency. He had screens placed around the ill man to preserve the last few shreds of his dignity, sent for a doctor, and brought the ball to an early close.

CHAPTER 8

The ladies rose only an hour after sunrise and partook of a hasty breakfast.

"Would you mind very much if I do not accompany you, dear?" Miss Bragg said. "I would like to do a little shopping."

"Not at all, Aurora. I know you do not like the heat overmuch and it looks as if today will be very warm. It was wise of Sir Robert to suggest such an early start. Indeed, I have never known him to be so thoughtful."

"Time mellows many a rash gentleman, I believe."

"In what way was Sir Robert rash?" Marianne asked, intrigued. "He seems very attentive and gentlemanly to me."

Fortunately for Lady Brancaster, Milton just then announced the gentlemen's arrival.

Lord Cranbourne drove Sir Horace, leaving Sir Robert a free space in his curricle. Perhaps unwilling to field any more questions from her outspoken niece, she accepted his invitation to ride with him, leaving Marianne and Georgianna alone in the barouche.

After they had passed through a turnpike at the edge of the town, they turned a bend in the winding road and a wide vista spread before them. A fertile plain led to a range of softly undulating hills, the odd church spire peeping between them. To their left, the Malvern Mountains soared in the distance. Whilst appreciating the beauty of the landscape, Marianne's attention was as ephemeral as the early morning mist that obscured their lofty peaks.

"Sir Robert is in love with Aunt Fanny, I think," she finally murmured. "Do you think she will have him?"

"Perhaps. But has it occurred to you that Lady Brancaster does not need a husband? She appears to be well off, after all."

"My uncle left her very well provided for," confirmed Marianne. "But I do not think Aunt Fanny is meant to be alone."

Georgianna's gaze was as clear and cool as a summer's sea. "She is not alone. She has Miss Bragg to keep her company."

Marianne's brow puckered as she considered this. "Yes, but it is not the same. I think Aunt Fanny needs to feel adored and protected. I have not seen her as happy as she appears to be in Sir Robert's company for a long time. I wonder…"

Never one to waste words, Georgianna merely quirked an enquiring brow.

"I wonder if we are getting in the way of their courtship?"

Georgianna considered her words. A small satisfied smile finally curved her lips. "That explains it!"

"Explains what?"

"Why Lord Cranbourne has taken this sudden
interest in us, of course. We saw nothing of him after
that incident at the well until last night. Did you not
notice how quick Sir Robert was to take him up on his
offer to guide us?"

A slow smile lightened Marianne's thoughtful
countenance. "You are right. How could I have been
so stupid to not have seen it?"

Georgianna looked away at the passing countryside for a moment, then said in a quiet voice, "Like
Miss Bragg, I too have had some experience of being
an outsider, looking in. For example, although Lord
Cranbourne is trying to keep us amused so Sir Robert
can woo your aunt, I think you have piqued his interest, whereas his attentions towards me are quite
perfunctory."

Marianne laughed. "If I have, it is only because I
amused him with my thoughtless prattle. But no
matter, I will turn it to good use. I think it is a splendid
scheme."

They passed through the pretty village of Prest-
bury and turned down a small lane. Here a most
surprising sight greeted them. Set on a relatively small
parcel of land was a tea house called The Grotto. At
the top of the garden, set on a raised terrace was a
Chinese temple surrounded by a covered balcony.
Below it, one side of the garden was taken up by a
circular rustic building and on the other a tall stone
tower loomed over the flowers and shrubs that filled
the remaining space.

"How extraordinary," said Lady Brancaster, when Sir Robert had helped her down from his curricle.

"I am pleased you approve my choice, ma'am," Lord Cranbourne said. "The round building is decorated with a variety of shells, fossils, and stones from the local hills, and there is a fine view of the surrounding countryside to be had from the top of the tower for any visitors who have the energy to climb it."

"I think I will visit the temple and sit in the shade for a few moments." Lady Brancaster waved her fan languidly. "The day is already becoming insufferably hot."

Sir Robert wasted no time in taking her arm and leading her there.

"Fossils did you say?" Sir Horace seemed unusually alert. "I've always been fascinated by 'em. I can't explain why exactly, except I find it amazing that a creature that lived thousands of years ago might be perfectly preserved."

"I quite agree." Lady Georgianna's reply startled him; his eyes bulged slightly, but retracted a smidgeon when she smiled at him and said confidingly, "I hope this will remain our secret, Sir Horace, but I too am fascinated by them."

He suddenly pulled his shoulders back and glanced up at the statuesque lady beside him. "Are you by Jove? Well it just goes to show, you can never tell."

Lady Georgianna looked down at him, an unusually kindly expression turning her eyes from glacier blue to soft velvet. "You can never tell what, Sir Horace?"

"What anyone else is thinking," he beamed, proffering his free arm. "I may have come to Cheltenham for the waters, but I am coming to realise that I am benefitting from something far more valuable."

Georgianna's lips twitched as she graciously accepted his escort. "And what might that be?"

"An education!" he said abruptly. "Do you know, I thought all you young ladies were interested in was the latest fashions or snaffling a husband? Meeting Miss Montagu and yourself has opened my eyes."

He wasn't the only one to be thus affected. Marianne's had also widened with a combination of amusement and amazement.

"Do not tell me, Miss Montagu, that you have spent more than five minutes in Bamber's company without realising he is somewhat eccentric?" Lord Cranbourne smiled down at her.

"You should smile more often," she advised him kindly. "It suits you. It was not Sir Horace who surprised me, however, but Georgianna. She can be as haughty as you if someone does not please her."

One of his dark brows winged up.

"Yes, just like that," she dimpled.

Despite himself he laughed. "You are incorrigible, ma'am. Shall we join the others?"

"I would rather see the view from the top of the tower." She began to walk towards it.

"As you wish, but I warn you there must be at least a hundred steps."

Marianne looked over her shoulder. "Are you trying to discourage me? You won't you know. I am not afraid of a little exercise."

"I doubt very much you are afraid of anything, Miss Montagu," he murmured dryly, following her through the archway at the base of the tower.

Lord Cranbourne had not exaggerated the number of steps and her legs were trembling by the time they reached the top, but it was worth it. The verdant vale stretched before them, dotted with corn-fields, woods, rivers, and villages – the whole bounded by the Welsh mountains, which were lilac smudges on the horizon.

"I hope the view meets your expectations, Miss Montagu."

Her eyes remained fixed upon it. "It exceeds them," she murmured softly. "It is at times like these that I wish I could paint."

"Did you bring some with you?"

She shook her head and sighed. "It would not matter if I had. Everything I paint always looks the same and never reflects my subject."

He gave a short bark of laughter. "Your honesty is refreshing, Miss Montagu. I am more used to the ladies of my acquaintance puffing off their accom-plishments, than admitting their failings."

Her hand went to the silver locket she wore. "My mother was very proficient in the art." She opened it and looked down at the miniature portrait that was set inside.

"Was?" he queried gently.

A small, wistful smile curved her lips. "She died five years ago."

"You have my sympathy, ma'am."

His softly uttered words held regret and she turned in surprise. "You have also suffered such a loss, I think."

"Indeed. May I?" He held out his hand.

"It is a self portrait," she said with some pride as

she placed it in his palm, the chain still about her neck.

He took a step closer, the better to examine it without the risk of snapping the delicate silver links. Only inches separated them. Marianne's eyes remained riveted on the large hand that held her locket and her cheeks began to burn as she suddenly felt the intimacy of the situation.

"She was very talented," he said softly. "She is a little darker than your aunt, but I can see the resemblance. You do not take much after her, at least, not in looks."

"No, I take after my father. My brother Simon is very like her though."

She felt a little breathless and the words came out in a whisper.

He gently closed the locket and let it fall back into place. When she continued to look down he tilted her chin with a crooked finger. His opaque gaze reminded her of shifting smoke.

"Your eyes are of the deepest, softest brown," he murmured. "A man could drown in them."

"Are you up there, Marianne?" Lady Brancaster's voice was faint but it acted like a douche of cold water.

Marianne took a swift step backwards and finally found her voice. "And so is a muddy puddle, sir, and a man could drown in that too!"

She turned swiftly on the words and leant over the rail. "Yes, Aunt Fanny. I am just coming."

Without looking in Lord Cranbourne's direction, she skirted around him and ran lightly down the stairs, one hand brushing the wall, the cold stone absorbing the uncomfortable heat that had so suddenly consumed her.

~

Lord Cranbourne looked out at the pretty scene before him for a moment, but it was a pair of wide soft eyes and a slightly parted mouth that he saw. Thank heavens Lady Brancaster had chosen that moment to interrupt them, for in another he would certainly have kissed those inviting lips. That would have been a very foolish mistake. He would either have had to declare himself or make himself scarce. He certainly had no wish to marry a girl who had no more to recommend her than a pert sense of humour and an unaffected manner. That he was also reluctant to call a halt to this charade just yet was understandable; he had promised Sir Robert a few days' grace and he liked to think that he was a man of his word

He had not been prepared for Miss Montagu's vulnerability when they had talked of her mother. He had meant to say something comforting, but all rational thought had fled when he had gazed into those innocently alluring eyes. A wry grin twisted his lips. However unoriginal his remark that a man could drown in her eyes had been, most young ladies would have lapped it up. But not Miss Montagu, she had given him his own again.

He would have to tread carefully with her for the rest of the day. It would be a shame if she clammed up on him, as it was her openness of manner that he enjoyed.

He guided the party next to a shady glade that

nestled beside the river Chelt and the baskets Sir Horace had brought were unpacked.

Lady Brancaster's eyes widened as she surveyed the huge array of fruit, meats, pies, and cakes he had ordered for their delectation.

"My goodness, Sir Horace. You have brought enough to feed a small army!"

"Thought I'd do the thing in style," he said simply. "I think everyone here will be able to find something they can enjoy."

"Of that you can be certain."

"You have indeed been very generous," Lady Georgianna said. "But we will never be able to eat the half of it. There will be so much waste."

He tapped one finger against his nose in a knowing way. "You're out there, ma'am. Anything left will go to the workhouse."

Lord Cranbourne looked at him in surprise. "You have thought of everything it seems, Bamber."

"It is a commendable idea," Marianne approved, seating herself beside him.

"Paid it a visit yesterday," he said.

"Good grief!" Sir Robert exclaimed. "Whatever for?"

"Some people, Robert," Lady Brancaster said coolly, "have more to think about than their own pleasure."

She turned a warm smile on Sir Horace. "That was very good of you. I seem to remember that your mother was involved with some committee or other, to improve conditions in such places."

"That's it, ma'am. I intend to write to her later and tell her all about it."

"Trying to get in her good books?" Lord Cranbourne said with a sardonic smile.

Marianne rose swiftly to his defence. "I think it an admirable thing to do, sir. Surely it is the duty of every gentleman of means to do something to help those less fortunate than himself?"

Lord Cranbourne bowed in her direction. "I stand corrected, ma'am," he said, his tone as cold as hers was hot.

"I should perhaps tell you, ma'am, that——"

"No, Bamber," Lord Cranbourne said softly. "You should never contradict a lady."

A rather awkward silence fell upon the party and once they had eaten their fill, it was decided that they should return.

"I, for one, am feeling quite fagged," Lady Brancaster said faintly.

Sir Robert helped her to her feet and led her towards his curricle but she came to a halt next to the barouche.

"I will travel back with the girls, Robert. I can put up the hood for some much needed shelter."

"Good idea, ma'am," said Sir Horace. "Would you mind if I squashed in beside you? Not feeling quite the thing meself."

When they arrived back in St George's Place, all the ladies were drooping somewhat. Miss Bragg immediately ordered a reviving pot of tea.

"I am not at all surprised you are all so flushed," she said. "It is the hottest day of the summer if I am not much mistaken."

"I am sure you are right, Aurora." Lady Brancaster leant back in her chair, kicked off her shoes, and raised her feet onto a footstool. "Did you find everything you required in town?"

"Indeed I did. The shops here are really very good. I ran into Mrs Skewitt in Mr Selden's. His shop is very elegant by the way, full of the sort of ornaments, jewellery, and perfume you might expect to find in Bond Street. Now, where was I?"

"Mrs Skewitt," Marianne prompted her.

"Oh yes, thank you, dear. Well, I thought it odd that Mrs Frobisher was not with her, for they always seem to go everywhere together. I enquired after her, of course, and discovered that she is extremely ill. Apparently with a similar illness to that poor man at the ball, last evening."

"Really?" Lady Brancaster murmured, clearly not very interested in the fate of Mrs Frobisher.

"But she is not the only one," added Miss Bragg. "Apparently a dozen people, at least, have been thus afflicted. It appears to be very contagious."

She finally had her employer's full attention. Lady Brancaster sat up abruptly. "Do not say so, Aurora. You know how susceptible I am to the least little thing."

"Indeed, my dear. But as you have not come down with anything yet, and have been out of town all day, I think you may escape it. I would suggest, however, that apart from a very early trip to the well, you remain indoors until we can be sure it is safe to circulate."

"Yes, I will take the waters, they may help strengthen my resistance to this mysterious disease. But girls, I insist you stay abed tomorrow. I will not give Frederick or Lady Westbury any reason to suppose I have not taken every care of you."

CHAPTER 9

Marianne had a restless night. The hot day was followed by an uncomfortably warm night. Time and again she threw off her bedcovers only to wake up some time later shivering as the sweat cooled on her skin. Before she could fall back into slumber, her various interactions with Lord Cranbourne would start preying on her mind.

She did not know what to make of him. Their meeting at the well had not left a favourable impression. He had been aloof and rude. At the ball, he had made more of an effort to please and she had enjoyed his company. But what disturbed her peace was that moment at the top of the tower. For those few suspended seconds she had felt herself to be completely in his power. She had been unable to move or think, and had felt a strange longing that she did not recognise.

Somewhere deep in the night, she had begun to understand why he might be called dangerous. How easy would it be for a girl to lose her reputation to such a one?

She awoke very early and padded over to the window. The sun peeped from behind the hills setting the sky ablaze with red and gold tints. With the arrival of dawn, her thoughts of the night before seemed exaggerated. They were, she realised, coloured by her own reactions. He had done nothing to compromise her and had she not invited him to flirt with her at the ball? He had shown no particular interest in her after-wards, especially after she had almost bitten his nose off for teasing Sir Horace. The following awkwardness had not helped Sir Robert's cause either. She sighed. If she were to promote her aunt's happiness, a cause that was very near to her heart, she must learn to curb her impetuous tongue.

The sudden scratching at her door was a welcome distraction. As she opened it, a streak of black shot into the room and under her bed.

"Duchess," she laughed. "You have escaped, you naughty cat."

She knelt on the floor and peered into the shad-ows. Two vibrant green eyes surveyed her warily.

"You are not happy?" she said softly. "Are you missing your home?"

The cat took a cautious step into the room, her tail between her legs and let out a low pitched yowl.

Marianne gently stroked its soft head but hastily retracted her hand when the fur beneath her fingers stood on end and it gave a warning hiss.

"I see. Lord Cranbourne thought you could find your own way, I wonder if he was right?"

She heard a soft click as the connecting door to

her dressing room opened.

"Miss Montagu, what are you doing up at this hour?"

Her maid spoke in hushed tones but still the cat darted back under the bed.

Marianne jumped decisively to her feet. "Nancy, I am going to let Duchess go."

"That cat's no more of a duchess than I am! She's the best mouser I've ever seen! Cook has become quite resigned to her presence even though she's a bad tempered little thing."

"That is why I am going to let her go. She is clearly unhappy. Only…"

Nancy eyed her warily. "I know that look of old, miss. You're up to some mischief, I'll be bound."

"No, really I'm not. But I need to be sure she can find it. I must follow her and perhaps explain to her owners why I took her."

Nancy crossed her arms and shook her head. "I knew it. You had just that look the night you pretended to be asleep and then sneaked out of the house for a moonlit stroll. Only problem was, you couldn't see in the dark and twisted your ankle in a rabbit hole! I will never forget the uproar when you weren't in your bed in the morning. You were lucky not to be carried off by an inflammation of the lung after laying in the garden all night!"

"Nancy! I was only thirteen!"

It had been not quite a year after her mother's death. She had still missed her sorely and, unwilling to burden her father with her unhappiness, had tried to bury it by voraciously reading her way through his library.

One afternoon, she had pulled a book out and an unbound manuscript had fallen to the floor. She had been intrigued when she saw that a Lady Montagu had written it. Her father had found her a few minutes later and whipped it out of her hands. She had been surprised, for he did not generally censor her reading. But on this occasion he had informed her that it was not appropriate and that she would not understand the half of it.

She had been reading *A Hymn to the Moon,* and had not found anything at all objectionable in it. Two lines had stuck in her mind: *By thy pale beams I solitary rove, To thee my tender grief confide.* She had decided to try it for herself.

The long hours she had lain on the grass had certainly given her ample opportunity to commune with the moon. She had not been frightened. It had been a warm summer's night and if it had not been for the pain in her swollen ankle, it would have been quite pleasant. She had stared at the night sky and allowed images of her mother to fill her thoughts. At one point, she had even thought she had felt her loving hand stroke her hair. When morning came she had felt tired but more at peace than she had in a long time.

"And then there was the time you—"

"Nancy, if you are going to recite all the madcap things I did as a child, we'll be here all day!"

"Well this start of yours is just as mad, and you don't have the excuse of being a child. Besides, Lady Brancaster will never permit it, not with this illness that's going around."

"That is why I am going to do it now, before

anyone is up. I am sure we will not have to go far. Do say you will come with me, Nancy. We will be back before anyone is any the wiser."

Nancy began to look resigned. "Oh, all right. You'll only go on your own if I don't. But we'll only follow for a short while, mind."

By the time Marianne was dressed and they had coaxed the cat out from under the bed, half an hour had passed.

"We must hurry," Marianne whispered as they quietly let themselves out of the front door.

Marianne set the cat down on the bottom step and she trotted off down the road without a backwards glance. They followed her onto High Street, but she soon turned into a narrow road bearing the title, Fleece Lane. The houses gradually became less salubrious and Nancy began to look unhappy.

"I don't like this, miss, not at all. I think we should turn back. This is no place for the likes of you."

"Just a few moments more, Nancy," Marianne pleaded.

They soon came to the edge of the town and the prospect opened. The cat did not hesitate, but leapt gracefully onto a field gate and then jumped down onto the grass beyond.

"Now, miss. I think we have gone far enough."

Marianne was already struggling with the latch. "I could understand your reticence when we were in those dark little lanes, Nancy. But there can be no harm in a tramp across a field or two. It is an age since I had a good walk. Now, hurry, or we will lose her and then I will never know what became of her."

Having been brought up in the country, Nancy

made sure the gate was shut before running after her mistress. She was somewhat out of breath when she finally caught up with her at the top of a short, steep rise.

"Look." Marianne beamed at her, pointing at a cluster of buildings down below. "There is a farm-house and it looks like Duchess is heading straight for it."

The series of buildings were set around a yard, and had held a rustic charm when viewed from afar, but on closer inspection they proved to be rather ramshackle. The barn had crumbling brickwork, the small stable was empty apart from a few chickens scrabbling in the dirt, and the roof of the farmhouse was more moss than straw. Duchess sat before a door that was rotten at the bottom, leaving a ragged gap of about four inches in one corner. Grime smeared a window that was cracked open a short way, but the faint glow of a lantern suggested someone was home.

As they carefully picked their way through the yard, which was strewn with various farm implements that looked as if they had been abandoned long ago, Duchess scratched at the door and announced her presence with a piteous miaow. It went unheard.

Marianne and Nancy froze as two strident voices screeched through the gap in the window.

"You'll be in for it now, you stupid lummox, and no mistake! People are dropping like flies they say."

"But I did it for us, Rose. I've been promised a handsome pay out. We'll be able to put this place to rights, or go somewhere else and start again."

"Promised a handsome pay out for dropping a dead sheep down the old well? I'll believe it when I see it. You 'ad better hope none of 'em crocks it or you'll be lucky if you don't end up dangling on the end of a rope!"

Nancy and Marianne began to back away, their wide eyes still fixed on the faint light that flickered behind the opaque window.

"We must get to the well before Aunt Fanny drinks the waters," Marianne hissed, urgently.

But even as she turned to run, her shins knocked painfully against a wooden plough that lay at a drunken angle. She was sent sprawling on the hard compacted earth of the yard. A short scream of surprise and pain escaped her before she could stop it.

The yelling suddenly stopped. She tried to scramble to her feet but the breath had been knocked from her.

"Go, Nancy," she gasped. "There is no time to lose."

The farmhouse door was warped, giving Nancy just enough time to dive behind the barn before it was wrenched open.

It was not every day that the occupants of the smallholding found a finely dressed lady sitting in their yard. Their mouths fell open in amazement. Marianne was not sure who was more shocked, they or her.

Deciding to try and brazen it out, she pasted a smile on her face. "Hello there. I am sorry to disturb you but I wonder if you have lost a cat?"

Duchess made a timely appearance and began to weave in and out of the woman's legs.

"There you are, you pesky cat. Where were you last night when the mice had the last of our bread?"

"Would you mind helping me up, sir?" Marianne

said. "You really ought to keep this yard more tidy you know. I could have suffered a serious injury."

"That I will, ma'am," he said striding purposefully forwards. "We wasn't expecting visitors, see."

Marianne gingerly took the rather grimy hand offered and found herself pulled quite roughly to her feet. She brushed at the bits of straw and dirt that had attached themselves to her dress.

"Thank you, sir. I found your cat hiding up a tree. A dog had chased it there. I put a notice in Mrs Jones's window but no one came for her."

The man gave her a leery grin, revealing a set of blackened teeth. Marianne had to resist the urge to cover her mouth as his foul smelling breath washed over her.

"The likes of me don't frequent such places, I'm afraid. On top of that, I can't read letters," he explained.

He made no move to step away and Marianne could not as the plough obstructed her way. She began to feel a little nervous.

"Yes, I see. Well, when nobody came I decided to see if she could find her own way home. I followed her just in case she could not, you understand. Now, if you will just step aside, my good man, I must be getting back or my aunt will begin to worry."

"I suppose she will," he agreed, a disturbingly sly look coming into his eyes. "Bein' as you're out so early and all alone, I don't suppose she knows what you're about."

His hand clamped around her arm. "Now you just come inside, missy. If you make no fuss, you'll come to no 'arm."

"But I don't want to come inside," she protested as he began dragging her towards the farmhouse.

"You should 'ave thought of that before you went poking your nose where it had no business bein'."

"I don't know what you mean," she squeaked, as he thrust her through the door into the farmhouse kitchen.

The fire had not been lit and the room was cold and dank, with ugly green smudges staining the thick walls. Marianne shivered as he pushed her into a roughly carved wooden chair and shook his head.

"Who'd o'thought such a refined lady as yourself would tell such a whopper? If you didn't hear us wrangling you must be deaf as a post."

Marianne began to see the gravity of her situation. She turned a look of appeal upon the lady of the house.

"Ma'am, you cannot mean to keep me here. Your situation will become far more serious if it becomes known you held a lady of quality here against her will. You must see that. Only this time, you will be culpable of a crime, also."

The woman pushed a hand through her already tangled locks and looked uncertainly at her husband.

"What do you intend to do, Josiah? I don't want no part in hurting a hair on her pretty little head."

Marianne let out a soft sigh of relief.

"Now don't you fret, my pet. I'm not such a lummox as you think. There's more in my cockloft than you know," he said, tapping his head.

His pet did not look convinced. Folding her arms across her greasy apron she sent him a sceptical look. "Well go on then, I can't read your mind."

"Has it occurred to you, Rose, that someone, somewhere, is going to be very anxious to retrieve this 'ere young lady? It wouldn't surprise me if they were to pay a substantial amount to get her back safe and sound."

A slow smile spread across his wife's face. "And if we were to get them to leave it somewhere else, we could be long gone afore they ever find her."

"You are wasting your time," Marianne assured them. "I will not give you my aunt's direction."

"You won't have to," Rose said, pulling on a rather ragged coat. "I can read well enough. I have to go into town to sell our eggs, anyways. It won't be no trouble to take a look in Mrs Jones's window. You keep a close eye on her, Josiah, I won't be long."

"Don't you worry, Rose, Miss Hoity Toity won't be goin' anywhere." He bent and opened a cupboard as he spoke. When he turned, he held a length of rope in his hands.

"It really isn't necessary," Marianne said, eyeing the thick, dirty rope a little apprehensively.

"So you say, miss. But it seems to me you're an unusually adventurous young lady, so I'll take no chances."

He bound her wrists tightly to the arms of the chair. Marianne winced as the rough rope bit into her tender skin.

When he was satisfied he took a step back and gave a mock bow. "You must forgive me for not enter-taining you, milady, but it seems as I've some packing to do."

As soon as the door closed behind him, Marianne struggled against her bonds, but he had done his job too well and the rope only chafed her slender wrists. She waited a few moments until his footsteps could no longer be heard before leaning forwards and bracing her feet. The chair was heavy and its legs grated against the stone floor as she dragged it to the door. She hooked one booted foot under the gap at the bottom and tugged at it but it refused to budge. A ragged laugh escaped her. She would not have got very far with a chair strapped to her, anyway, and what a sight she would have been.

She dropped her head and closed her eyes, willing the tears that threatened to recede. Why, oh why, had she not listened to Nancy or her aunt? Sighing, she straightened and took a deep breath. No, she was glad that she had not, for at least she had discovered the source of the illness that was spreading through the town. She would just have to be patient and wait to be rescued.

She bit her lip as a blur of movement caught her eye. Her love of animals did not extend to rats and this was a very large one. It paused for a moment and regarded her curiously. She gasped as it approached her. Stifling the scream that rose in her throat, she kicked out at it, and sagged in relief when it darted away and disappeared through the hole in the door.

"Duchess," she called softly. "Where are you? Is this how you reward me for seeing you safely home?" She glanced about her and sighed. "Perhaps you are right, it is not much of a home, is it? Not even a fire to keep you warm."

She would try to be patient, but please God, let them come soon.

CHAPTER 10

Lord Cranbourne and Sir Horace had returned to The George Inn to discover that three guests staying at the establishment had been struck down by the mysterious illness going around. The talk in the taproom was that it was spreading like wildfire.

"I've never known anything like it," Mr Randall, the proprietor, informed them glumly. "I've already had two regulars, who were booked in for a month, take to their heels. And you can be sure that others will follow 'em tomorrow."

Over a very good supper of mutton and trout they considered their options.

"I don't like it," Sir Horace said. "Not at all. It's a damn shame. They keep a fine table here and my foot is beginning to improve, but I think we should bid adieu to Cheltenham."

Lord Cranbourne did not immediately reply. He was aware of a vague feeling of dissatisfaction. Now that he had been presented with the perfect opportunity to flee Cheltenham without any loss of face, he felt somehow reluctant to do so, as if he were leaving behind unfinished business.

"You are right, of course," he finally said, frowning. "I suggest we look in on the pump room in the morning so we can take our leave of Lady Brancaster's party. I'd also like a word with Sir Robert. I promised him I'd be here until the end of the week. While I am sure he will understand, I wouldn't like to shab off without apologising."

"Good idea," Sir Horace agreed. "Wouldn't mind taking one last glass of the waters to see me on my way."

He suddenly frowned, dropped his head into his hands, and sighed deeply.

Lord Cranbourne's lips twitched. "Out with it, Bamber. What has just occurred to you?"

Sir Horace reached for his glass and took a restorative swig of wine. "Never could get anything past you, Cranbourne. It was when I said, 'my way', that it struck me."

Lord Cranbourne raised an eyebrow. "I hope I won't lower myself in your esteem, Bamber, but I'm afraid I'll need a little more to go on if I am to understand you."

"Can't go home yet, my cousin is there for a few more days yet."

"Surely you are not afraid of your mother, Bamber? She is one of the nicest women of my acquaintance. I really cannot imagine her forcing you to do anything you do not wish to."

"Not force me, no. But it's not my wishes that are the problem – it is hers. Feel like a savage every time I disappoint her. One of these days I'm bound to cave in. But not with my cousin."

"No, if she has both a squint and buck teeth, she is not to be considered. But if you do not wish your mother to choose for you, you must look about you yourself. A very wise woman once said to me, that unless you at least open your mind to the possibility, you are very unlikely to find someone who will suit."

Sir Horace looked at him a little resentfully. "And have you followed this wise woman's advice?"

Lord Cranbourne gave a rueful grin. "You have me there, Bamber."

Sir Horace's usual good humour was restored. "By Jove, I have, haven't I? Must be the first time! I suppose I'll find a cosy little inn somewhere and tuck myself away for the week. Care to join me?"

"No, dear fellow. I do not."

"Thought as much," Sir Horace said gloomily.

Lord Cranbourne rose to his feet and smiled gently down at his old friend. "We would both be heartily bored before the week was out. There would be nothing to do but eat, drink, and play cards. *If* the waters here have benefited you in some small way, you would find all the good undone before the week was out. You had better come with me to Cranbourne."

Sir Horace's eyes grew round with amazement. "Cranbourne? But the Ponsonby chit!"

Lord Cranbourne shrugged. "I am sure my estate is large enough that we can make ourselves scarce. We will only have to bear with Maria's guests for another week, after all. So, do you come, Bamber?"

"Sorry, old chap. Grateful for the invite and all that, but it is too close to home. Wouldn't be surprised if mother paid a visit and if she discovered I was there, I would be in a hobble. Wouldn't ring a peal over me, just give me that hurt look that makes me feel like a regular blackguard."

Lord Cranbourne smiled wryly. "I understand only too well, my friend. And I have to concede that there is every chance that Lady Bamber will call on my sister, as it would only be polite for her to do so. What about your brother?"

Sir Horace looked much struck by this suggestion. "Of course! Haven't seen Loftus for an age and he is the best of good fellows."

Lord Cranbourne couldn't agree more. He was intelligent and scholarly, but with a wit and humour that he suspected was rarely seen now that he had taken orders. It was fortunate that he had been the second born son, for unlike Bamber, he was well equipped to fend for himself.

"Near Dorchester isn't he?" Lord Cranbourne said.

"Priddletown," Sir Horace confirmed.

"I will take you as far as Salisbury, then. You can hire a chaise from there."

Sir Horace beamed at him. "Didn't I say you were the best of good fellows?"

"You may not think so when I tell you I intend to be at the well by six o'clock." He eyed Sir Horace's nattily tied neckcloth. "As I would hazard a guess that it takes your valet at least an hour to achieve your preferred state of sartorial elegance, I suggest you forgo the port and get yourself to bed."

If they did not quite make the appointed time, they arrived at the well not more than ten minutes after it. Even at that early hour, there was already a smattering of visitors. As they strolled into the square they saw Sir Robert sat on a bench in front of the long room. His hands were thrust deep into his pockets, his long legs stretched out before him, and his gaze was firmly fixed on the archway that gave entrance from the well walk.

After greeting him, Sir Horace wandered off to join the small queue waiting to receive their glass of water.

Sir Robert was not surprised to hear that Lord Cranbourne and Sir Horace were leaving.

"I will own myself amazed if Lady Brancaster does not quickly follow suit," he said, solemnly.

"Perhaps you could persuade her to remove to Bath?" Lord Cranbourne suggested.

Sir Robert's countenance lightened, but only for an instant. "All the best lodgings will already be taken," he said gloomily.

"Well at least you will have her to yourself this morning, for apart from a footman, she is quite unattended."

Sir Robert sprang to his feet as the footman stepped forwards and helped her alight from a sedan chair. She emerged in a flutter of fine muslin and lace.

Sir Robert crossed the square hastily and bowed low over her hand. "I hoped you would come. I should have known your courage would not be daunted by this strange sickness."

"But I am daunted, Robert. And I shall not stay long for I must decide what to do. If it were only myself I had to consider things might be different. But I cannot and will not put Marianne or Lady Georgianna at risk. Frederick would never forgive me, nor would I forgive myself if I were to let anything befall Marianne. I promised him I would take the greatest care of her."

"And you have, my dear." He looked a little rueful. "No one is more aware of it than I, but might I suggest that—"

He broke off as the unprecedented sight of a maid running full pelt into the square caught their attention. She came to an abrupt halt, glanced wildly around taking great gulps of air, before picking up her skirts again and flying across the remaining space between them.

"Nancy!" exclaimed Lady Brancaster, startled, as she noted her heated cheeks and panicked expression. "Calm yourself, please. I do believe every eye is upon you!"

"I'm sorry, ma'am," she gasped, clutching her side. "But the situation is urgent! It's Miss Montagu! She's in trouble."

Lady Brancaster's hand flew to her cheek.

Lord Cranbourne caught the words as he strolled up to them. His brow furrowed.

"Out with it!" he said, in an urgent undertone. "What has she done now?"

The morning's escapade tumbled from Nancy's lips. "I'm that sorry," she said on a sob. "I tried to stop her, but she would insist she must make sure it found its way."

"Never mind that," snapped Lord Cranbourne. "Were you seen?"

Nancy shook her head. "No, sir. I hid behind the barn."

He nodded briskly. "Then we have the advantage. Do you think you can show me the way?"

The maid nodded eagerly.

"Then we must not delay." He turned to Lady Brancaster. "Please inform the pump woman that she must not let anyone drink from the well…" he paused, his eyes widening. "Bamber!"

They all turned. Sir Horace had just reached the head of the queue. Lord Cranbourne rushed across the square, pushing anyone in his way aside. Ignoring the startled cries and oaths directed at him, he reached his friend just as he raised the glass to his lips. He dashed it aside. Airborne droplets of water glinted in the sun for a moment before falling to the hard, thirsty ground, where the glass lay shattered. The hubbub was replaced by a stunned silence.

Lord Cranbourne's low deep tones rang out. "No one else must drink from the well. If you already have, I suggest you seek medical advice."

He turned to the woman who drew the water. "I have been informed that there is a dead sheep in your well."

Having dropped this bombshell into the silence, he did not wait to field the inevitable questions his words would generate, but strode purposefully back to Nancy.

"I will take you up in my curricle, there is no time to waste."

Taking her by the arm, he hurried away with her.

The autocratic manner in which Lord Cranbourne had taken charge of the situation, rankled Sir Robert. The opportunity to finally serve Lady Brancaster in a matter of some import had been seemingly snatched out of his hands. Unwilling to lose the chance to show himself in a good light, he said, "Come, Fanny. I shall take you in my curricle. Have no fear, I will ensure Marianne is safely restored to you."

Lord Cranbourne had a start on him, but only the finest whips were admitted to the four-horse club and he used all his consummate skill to catch him. Only the knowledge that he could drive to an inch prevented Lady Brancaster from calling out when he feather-edged a corner or held close to a sharp bend.

"This takes me back, Fanny," he murmured as they turned onto a cart track.

"That is old history, Robert. I would not have agreed to this madcap chase if things had not been desperate."

He glanced down at her tenderly. "And I would not have subjected you to it, then or now, if things had not been desperate, of that you can be certain."

Their eyes held for a long moment. Recovering first, Lady Brancaster looked resolutely ahead and shrieked. "Robert!"

Lord Cranbourne had pulled up beside a farm gate that hung half off its hinges, giving access to a small farmyard. Only an iron fist upon the reins enabled Sir Robert to bring his horses to an abrupt halt with barely a moment's notice.

"Stay here, Fanny," he said peremptorily.

"No, Robert," she said with cool dignity. "Either you will help me down, or I shall jump down myself."

Muttering under his breath something about stubborn creatures, he reluctantly aided her to alight.

"At least stay back until we see how things stand," he said urgently.

"Oh, very well, but hurry."

Lord Cranbourne nodded towards the yard as he approached and laid one finger to his lips. They peered around the hedge as a woman climbed over the stile on the far side of the yard. If she had but looked in their direction once, she would have seen the horses' heads poking above the hedge. Fortunately, she seemed preoccupied and strode towards the house without once glancing towards the track.

As soon as she disappeared into the farmhouse, they picked their way quietly through the cluttered yard and crouched stealthily under the window.

"I've packed up our things, Rose. 'Ave you found out where our guest's aunt lives?"

"I have," came the short reply.

"Where have you told her to leave the readies?"

"Patience, Josiah. That 'as always been your problem, you're always rushing headlong into things without considering the consequences. You told me your uncle had left you a nice bit 'o property and off we trot, only to find ourselves in this sorry old place. You shove our last sheep down that well, just 'cos someone tells you he'll make it worth yer while without a thought as to why he wanted you to do it. It may be that your latest scheme might lift us out o' the mire we've fallen in to, but only if we tread carefully. We'll wait 'til tomorrow to make our demands. By then this aunt of hers will be worriting proper."

"I am sorry for your misfortune." Marianne's subdued voice drifted through the window. "But you are only going to make your situation worse if you keep me here. Let me go and I will happily give you what little money I have by me."

Lord Cranbourne tensed as if to move but found an iron grip around his wrist. Sir Robert shook his head. "You don't know if they are armed, you fool," he whispered.

"That's mighty kind of you, miss," Rose said. "And if we weren't in such dire straits, I might do just that."

"Then at least untie me," Marianne pleaded. "This rope is burning into my wrists."

That was all Lord Cranbourne needed to hear. He was up in an instant. He moved quickly to the door and lashed out at it with one booted foot. Sir Robert was close behind him.

One swift glance assured him that Sir Robert's concern was unwarranted. A man slouched in a chair by the table, the woman he had seen so recently enter the room, stood beside him. Ignoring them, Lord Cranbourne strode swiftly to Marianne and dropped to one knee, pulling a small knife from an inner pocket of his coat.

"I'll have you free in an instant," he growled.

"Thank you," she whispered.

The grating of wood against stone jarred the air as Josiah pushed himself hastily to his feet and lunged at him. He found himself propelled backwards by a huge hand that had appeared as if from nowhere and clamped itself around his arm. Josiah was a strong man who had had to fight his way out of many a tricky situation, but he was unbalanced and even as he swung wildly at the stranger who suddenly loomed before him, he received a crunching blow to his nose and crumpled to the ground in an inanimate heap.

Rose wasted no time in weeping and wailing over her afflicted husband, but darted out of the door. Lady Brancaster had waited only until she saw Lord Cranbourne and Sir Robert disappear inside the farmhouse before following them. With great presence of mind, she put out one daintily shod foot as Rose rushed past her. She watched with some satisfaction as she went sprawling in the dirt. Not to be outdone and feeling the need to make some amends, Nancy promptly sat upon her. As the cook at Harwich Court was a dab hand at puddings, and Nancy had a very sweet tooth, she was no longer as slight as she had once been, so her method of restraint whilst somewhat crude, proved very effective.

"Get off me you great lump, I can't breathe," Rose gasped.

"Serves you right," Nancy said. "You deserve everything that's coming to you!"

Sir Robert appeared in the doorway. "Let her up," he said coolly.

As she staggered to her feet, he stood aside and nodded for her to enter the farmhouse.

"It's not my fault," she whined as she passed him. "None of it's my fault. It's all his doing." She prodded her unconscious spouse with her foot. "And nothing bad has happened to the young lady, after all."

"You call this nothing?" Lord Cranbourne said harshly. "Look at her!"

All eyes turned for a moment to the ugly red welts that marked Marianne's wrists.

"Oh, my poor dear." Lady Brancaster flew around the table to her side.

"It is partly my fault," admitted Marianne. "I tried

to loosen the rope by twisting against it."

"That was none of my doin' neither," Rose said.

"Save your breath for the parish constable and the magistrate," Lord Cranbourne snapped. "They might be interested in your excuses, I am not."

Rose's eyes flashed. "No, your sort is only interested in your finery and pleasure. What do you care that the rest of us are left to scratch about in the dirt? The price of your coat alone would feed us for a year or more. I know that keeping her here was wrong, but we are desperate and we wouldn't have done her no harm."

"They were going to ask for money in return for my release," Marianne said.

A sly gleam of intelligence suddenly brightened Rose's eyes. "But we haven't, we only held you here. I am sorry Josiah tied you up so tight, miss, but you might want to consider that, if you bring any sort of case against us, it will be reported in the papers."

Lady Brancaster sank into a nearby chair. "She is right. And although you acted with the best of intentions, Marianne, spiteful people will speculate as to what happened to you in the time you were held here. Not to mention why you were roaming around the countryside at this early hour with only your maid in attendance."

"I do not wish to bring a case against you," Marianne said quietly. "But I am not the only one affected by your actions. Many people are very ill."

The fight seemed to go out of Rose, but in a moment she rallied. "My Josiah is not a bad man," she insisted. "But he hasn't got much between his ears. He was told he would be paid 'andsome to drop a sheep down that well. He didn't think no further than that. But he is not to blame, not really. It is the one as asked him to do it who is the real villain."

"Although I hate to say it," Sir Robert said, "she is right." He glanced at the prone man. "Throwing him in the lock-up will serve no purpose, apart from putting the real culprit on his guard."

"Thank you, sir." Rose sank down beside Josiah as he groaned.

"Not so fast," Sir Robert continued. "I think the local magistrate will be very interested in what he has to say."

"But, sir—"

"I think you will find that if he is honest, and no one suffers anything worse than an upset stomach, he will be treated with some leniency." He glanced at Lady Brancaster. "And if he keeps Miss Montagu's name out of his account, I will even plead his case."

"Oh, Robert," Lady Brancaster sighed. "Thank you."

He turned to Lord Cranbourne. "Would you mind taking Lady Brancaster and Miss Montagu back to St George's Place whilst I see to it? I met Mr Merritt at a ball last week and know his direction."

"Of course not." Lord Cranbourne smiled apologetically at Nancy. "I am afraid there will be no room for you."

A look of relief crossed her face. She had found the dash through the lanes at breakneck speed quite terrifying. "I'd as lief walk anyways, sir. It's only a short way across the fields."

Rose gave her a darkling look. "The exercise will do you good."

CHAPTER 11

The short drive to St George's Place was accomplished in silence. Marianne knew that her aunt would not embarrass her in front of Lord Cranbourne, but she had not expected such consideration from him. She was grateful for it, for now her ordeal was over she felt quite subdued and more than a little shaky.

Lord Cranbourne helped them down from his curricle and bowed. "It has occurred to me that I left Sir Horace in rather an awkward situation. I must go to him. If you do not object, Lady Brancaster, we will return here and await the outcome of Sir Robert's interview with the magistrate."

"Of course, Lord Cranbourne. And please accept my thanks for all you have done this morning."

He bowed and climbed back into his curricle. He had an inkling that he would find Sir Horace back at the inn and his instincts did not deceive him. Despite the early hour he had a glass of claret in his hand. His appearance was unusually dishevelled. His neckcloth was askew as if he had been repeatedly tugging at it, and his usually perfectly coiffured locks were wildly disarranged.

He jumped to his feet as soon as Lord Cranbourne entered the room and strode over to him, his chin jutting out in a belligerent manner, and his green eyes darkening with an anger that was quite alien to his character.

"Cranbourne! You deserve I should call you out! What a scurvy trick you played on me! If it was your idea of a joke, I will take leave to inform you that it was not at all amusing!"

Never in their long acquaintance had Lord Cranbourne seen his friend in such a taking. He placed a gentle hand on his shoulder and gave it a small squeeze.

"Calm yourself, Bamber. It was no joke. I am sorry that I left you in such a predicament but the case was urgent, I assure you."

Sir Horace's eyes widened. "Do you mean to tell me there really is a dead sheep at the bottom of that well?"

"Yes, my friend."

Sir Horace looked a little mollified, but then his colour heightened. "It is outrageous! I was within ames ace of drinking that water!"

"Exactly so," murmured Lord Cranbourne.

"Well, I am dashed glad you stopped me, but why did you rush off in that scrambling way? Everyone turned on me and began to bombard me with questions. Wouldn't believe I didn't know what you were talking about."

"Poor, Bamber," Lord Cranbourne said softly. "Was it very bad?"

"It was worse than bad, it was a nightmare! I jumped into a sedan chair and told 'em I'd make it worth their while if they got me out of there post haste."

"Very wise. Sit down, Bamber, and I will tell you all."

Sir Horace listened with rapt attention as he unfolded his tale. Lord Cranbourne was surprised and relieved that he refrained from uttering various interjections as was his habit, and even more surprised by his reaction when he came to the end of it. Considering his admiration of Miss Montagu, he expected outraged exclamations, but on the contrary, his friend was very measured in his response.

"She's a dashed fine gal," he said. "Very kind hearted, but rash, very rash. She must have seemed like the goose that laid the golden egg to that poor, misguided couple."

"You are more generous than I," Lord Cranbourne said. "That poor, misguided couple caused her much discomfort and have given her enough food to feed many a nightmare."

"Ah, but food is at the very heart of the matter, Cranbourne. A starving man or woman can easily be led into folly. Crime or the workhouse are sometimes their only options and most workhouses are still only one step up from a prison. I feel dashed sorry for Miss Montagu, not to mention all those who are ill, but it is easy for those of us who have plenty to judge those who have nothing. Miss Montagu has suffered a hard lesson today, but it may do her some good. She is too trusting, and that can also lead to folly."

Lord Cranbourne gave his friend a long, considering stare. "You may be right, Bamber. I have underestimated you, I think. I have just realised that I too might be guilty of the folly of being too trusting," he said softly.

"You! Too trusting! Hardly, dear chap."

"You think not? I would until a very few moments ago have agreed with you. Indeed, I would even have gone as far as to say I prided myself on not being gulled."

Sir Horace looked bemused. "Who has gulled you?"

Lord Cranbourne leaned forwards and pointed a finger. "You, you charlatan."

"I don't know what you mean!" Sir Horace spluttered.

"Stubble it, Bamber. It has just occurred to me that when I entered this room, you jumped out of that chair and strode up to me without even a hint of a limp. You've been shamming it, you shameless fraud."

Sir Horace looked uncomfortable and shifted awkwardly in his chair. "Sorry, old fellow. But I had to give mother some excuse for coming to take the waters. Seemed best to stick to the same story with everyone; you know I have a wretched memory. Besides, I needed some excuse not to dance at the assemblies."

Lord Cranbourne relaxed back in his chair and began to laugh. "You, Bamber, are a card. And to think you have been drinking those foul tasting waters for nothing. No wonder you felt better on the days you did not attend the well."

Looking a little shamefaced, Sir Horace went to the mirror that hung above the fireplace. His brows rose in horror as he saw the damage he had done to his neckcloth. He hastily began to rectify it.

"Ah, so the artistry is all yours, Bamber. And I thought you left everything to your valet," murmured Lord Cranbourne, getting to his feet. "You are full of surprises."

"A man must know how to tie his own neckcloth," Sir Horace said. "A valet cannot always be relied upon. Ours must be well on the way to Salisbury by now along with our baggage. I suggest we follow them, smartish."

"We will, but first we must call on Lady Brancaster. You would not like to depart without taking your leave of her and her guests, I am sure."

Sir Horace considered his friend with a wary eye. "I'd rather the ladies remained in ignorance of my little hoax if it's all the same to you, Cranbourne."

He glanced down at his friend, a sardonic gleam in his eyes. "Very well, Bamber. But only because I do not wish to cause Miss Montagu any more disillusionment than she has already suffered this day."

Milton opened the door before Lady Brancaster and Marianne had mounted the first step, his face grave.

"Miss Bragg and Lady Georgianna are in the morning room, ma'am."

"Thank you, Milton. Inform them I will meet

them in the drawing room in a few minutes. We are expecting visitors. If Sir Robert, Lord Cranbourne, or Sir Horace Bamber arrive, show them up immediately, we are not at home to anyone else."

"Very well, ma'am."

Lady Brancaster took Marianne straight to her bedchamber. It was the largest of the bedrooms and doubled as her private sitting room. She led Marianne to a sofa set before the fireplace and gently bathed her wrists with vinegar.

Marianne sucked in her breath and winced.

"I am sorry, my love, but that rope looked very dirty. It will only sting for a moment."

She wandered over to her dressing table and surveyed the many small pots that littered it for a moment. "Ah, the alkanet ointment, I think."

She gently rubbed the ointment into the ugly red welts that marked Marianne's wrists. "This will soothe them."

"I am sorry, Aunt Fanny," she said in a small voice.

Lady Brancaster glanced up at her, her eyes unusually serious. "What is it that you are sorry for, Marianne? Going against my wishes, getting found out, causing me a great deal of worry, or very nearly embroiling yourself in the most unsavoury of scandals?"

Although her aunt's voice was gentle, Marianne's eyes shimmered with tears.

"All of them. I-I didn't see the harm—"

"You never do," Lady Brancaster said. "And although every generation feels it knows better than the one that went before, it is time you learned that your elders are wiser than you. You are a very green girl, Marianne. You know nothing of the world yet and must allow yourself to be advised by those who do."

Unused to hearing her aunt talk to her in such a stern tone, the tears overflowed, running silently down her pale cheeks.

Lady Brancaster's eyes softened, she bent towards her niece as if to embrace her but then paused, straightened, and crossed again to her dressing table. Opening a small drawer, she retrieved a handkerchief and a pair of gloves and offered them to Marianne. "A good cry will probably relieve your feelings and these gloves will cover your wrists. I shall be in the drawing room when you have collected yourself."

As soon as the door closed softly behind her, Marianne buried her face in the handkerchief to quieten the wrenching sobs that racked her. Lady Brancaster's disapproval weighed heavy on her heart. To have earned such censure from the one who most closely reminded her of her mother brought her to a realisation of just how foolish she had been. She had, she realised, been blinded by hubris. She had acted in a way she knew her aunt would have disapproved of because she felt it was the right thing to do, but also because she prided herself on her intelligence and judgement – a judgement that had proved to be sadly lacking.

These melancholy reflections led her to consider her behaviour over the last year. Her ruminations did not bring her any comfort and she rapidly descended into a barrage of self-recrimination. She had persuaded herself that she was making things easier for her father by agreeing to attend Miss Wolfraston's

Seminary, but she had gone because she was unprepared to do the one thing that would really have made him happy; forge some sort of relationship with his wife.

She had resented any interference in the comfortable routine that had been established between herself and her father over the years, and had not hesitated to contradict or ignore anything her stepmother had said if it did not tally with her own wishes. Nor had she hesitated in airing her grievances to her aunt and colouring her view of Lady Montagu.

She groaned. Her stepmother had been a spinster who had been left firmly on the shelf. To be suddenly thrust into the role of wife and mother could not have been easy. If Aunt Fanny did not send her straight back home after today's debacle, when she next wrote home she would direct the letter to her.

She glanced up as someone knocked on the door. Georgianna poked her head around it. "Do you mind if I come in?"

"Not at all." Marianne offered her a rather wan smile. "I suppose you have heard that I am in disgrace."

Georgianna closed the door softly behind her. "I think you will be forgiven once Lady Brancaster gets over the shock of this morning's events. Miss Bragg has pointed out to her that although your actions were perhaps not very wise, you have saved a great many more people from becoming ill."

"Good old Miss Bragg," Marianne murmured.

Georgianna sat down beside her. "Were you quite terrified?"

Marianne gave a shaky laugh. "Only by a rat. I

somehow knew that my captors didn't really mean me any harm. And I knew I would be rescued before too long."

"And so you were, by Lord Cranbourne," Georgianna murmured. "For the second time. I hope you were more polite to him on this occasion."

The blush that stained Marianne's cheeks added some much needed colour to her pale complexion.

"Apparently he acted with commendable promptitude."

"And I am very grateful to him," Marianne acknowledged. "And also to Sir Robert, who aided him very competently."

A thoughtful look clouded her eyes and a slow smile curved her lips. "Indeed, he took charge of the situation in a very impressive manner once I had been released."

"Yes, Lady Brancaster did mention that she felt very obliged to him."

They were interrupted by Nancy.

"You're both wanted in the drawing room," she said. "But you best go and wash your face first, Miss Montagu, if you don't want everyone to know you've been weeping." Her eyes fell to her raiment. "And you'd best hurry for we'll need to change your dress too. It's covered in dust, straw, and something else I really don't care to think about."

Sir Horace and Lord Cranbourne had arrived by the time Marianne went down. She returned their bows and thanked Lord Cranbourne very prettily for his aid before seating herself next to her aunt.

A slightly awkward silence fell upon the room. Although nobody present wished to embarrass Marianne or cause her any further distress, the events of the day loomed large in everyone's mind and any other topic of conversation seemed too trivial to mention.

"You must give your mother my best wishes," Miss Bragg finally said to Sir Horace.

"I will, of course. But I am going first to visit my brother."

"Oh, you are leaving?" Although Marianne's words addressed Sir Horace, her eyes slipped to his companion.

"We are," confirmed Lord Cranbourne. He glanced enigmatically at his friend. "Sir Horace finds his foot much improved."

"I am glad to hear it." She was aware of a sinking sensation in her stomach.

Milton announced Sir Robert and they all stood.

"Is it settled?" Lady Brancaster asked.

"My part in it is, at all events," Sir Robert said. "Mr Merritt has taken the wider view of the situation, as I thought he would. He is most concerned about the town's reputation. But the situation is extremely tricky."

"How so?" Lady Brancaster asked.

"If the owner of the well insists on bringing an action against the perpetrator of the offence, which in all likelihood will be one of his competitors, then he must prove their involvement. The puppet who carried out the act, was given the instruction by an intermediary, who has by all accounts disappeared."

"Do you mean to say that nothing can be done?" Lady Brancaster said, outraged.

"No, I do not say that. All of the wells are to be

closed whilst further investigations are carried out and the quality of their water checked. A meeting of all the well owners will be attended by several persons of local eminence who will make it known that if any other cases of suspected sabotage occur, there will be serious consequences, yet to be decided, for all."

"And what will happen to Josiah?" Marianne asked quietly.

"Fortunately for him, Mr Merritt was of the opinion that it could only further damage the town's reputation, on which its prosperity depends, if any rumour of sabotage were to circulate. It would bring into question the integrity of all the well owners and could benefit no one. It will be given out that it was an unfortunate accident. As for Josiah and his wife, I think you will find that they have joined the throng of people who are fleeing Cheltenham in droves."

"And who could blame them?" Lady Brancaster sighed. "I have hired this house for another month, but if it were not for the fact that we now know the source of the problem and no longer need fear becoming ill ourselves, I would follow them. I must say that I am still tempted, Cheltenham has suddenly lost its charm."

Sir Robert's brows drew together in a frown.

"Perhaps I might offer a suggestion?" Lord Cranbourne said. "My sister, Lady Strickland, is at present presiding over a small house party at my estate in Wiltshire. I was on my way there when I stopped at the well to take my leave of you. I would like to extend an invitation to all of your party, Lady Brancaster, and to you, of course, Sir Robert, to join me there."

"How very generous of you," Lady Brancaster

said. "But I hesitate to impose on you when you have already been so very helpful to us."

Lord Cranbourne's lips twisted into a wry smile. "I fear I must come clean." He glanced at Marianne and thought he saw a look of hope in her eyes. "It was my pleasure to help Miss Montagu out of the difficult predicament she found herself in. What is more, I was honour bound to do so, for I was in some measure, responsible for it."

Lady Brancaster gasped. "But how can that be so?"

"It was I who put the idea of letting the cat find its own way home, into her head. I would not have done so, however, if I had realised she would follow it." His eyes again dwelled on Marianne for a moment. "But on reflection, even though our acquaintance is of short duration, I think my failure to predict that possibility, shows a quite distressing lack of foresight on my part."

Lady Brancaster pondered his words for a moment. "You must not think I hold you responsible in any way, Lord Cranbourne, but I do think your idea has some merit. There is bound to be a degree of speculation as to why Marianne's maid rushed into the square in such a panic this morning, and as to why we all left in such a hurry."

"You are very right, my dear," Miss Bragg agreed. "And I do believe the old adage, 'out of sight, out of mind' is a wise one."

"Indeed." Lady Brancaster eyed Lord Cranbourne thoughtfully. "Who else will be there?"

He gave a rueful smile. "I am not at all sure. I know Lord Ponsonby and his family have been invited, and I suppose Lord Strickland might have one or two of his friends down. As I had not meant to attend, I did not take much interest in my sister's arrangements."

"I had heard Miss Lucinda Ponsonby had made her come out," Lady Brancaster said casually. "She is reported to be quite a beauty."

"She is," interjected Sir Horace. "Yellow blonde hair and blue eyes. Reminds me of one of the porcelain figures my mother likes so much."

"Let us hope that she is not quite as delicate." Lady Brancaster smiled. "We will accept your offer, Lord Cranbourne. We will be a day behind you, that way Lady Strickland will not be taken completely by surprise. Besides, I really do not feel up to any more excitement today."

After they had taken their leave, Milton presented to Miss Bragg a small silver salver upon which lay a calling card.

"A Mrs Skewitt called, wishing to see you, ma'am." Although his face remained as impassive as ever, something in his tone indicated he did not rate Mrs Skewitt very highly.

"Thank you, Milton." She took the card and sighed. "I think the speculation has already begun."

"You will not visit her, Aurora, surely?" Lady Brancaster said. "She is one of the worst gossips it has ever been my misfortune to encounter."

"Oh no, dear. But I shall write her a letter and enquire after her sister's health. I shall say that I am sure she will understand that we have decided to leave town for a short while until this dreadful sickness passes. Indeed, I shall even suggest we had intended to attend a small house party all along and promise to call on her with all our news when we return."

"That is very kind of you, Aurora, but I really do not see why you should put yourself to so much trouble. I cannot think that she merits such civility. Milton is quite capable of dealing with her should she come calling again."

"Oh yes, of course," she said. "But I think in this case, it would be better to appease her, just a little. If we do not give her some reason for our sudden departure, I feel sure she will fabricate one. But armed with this snippet of information, she will enjoy pooh poohing any ridiculous rumours that might circulate as malicious gossip, whilst enjoying all the consequence of being in our confidence."

CHAPTER 12

They were two days on the road. The first passed quite quickly, each of the travellers feeling the excitement and anticipation of visiting a new place. They broke their journey at The Angel in Wootton Bassett, enjoying a dinner superior to the average fare a traveller might expect at a coaching inn, and finding the sheets well aired and the beds comfortable, enjoyed a satisfying night's repose.

As they journeyed further south, signs of habitation became less frequent. Gently undulating countryside dotted with sheep spread before them, only the occasional oddly shaped mound breaking the monotony of the view. It was pleasant enough but held nothing of sufficient interest to hold the observer's attention for long.

Marianne became restless and retrieved a sheet of paper and a pencil from her reticule. After a few moments' thought, she began to scribble a few words upon it.

"If you wish to write a letter, my dear, might I

suggest you wait until we reach Cranbourne? Although my carriage is very well sprung, I cannot imagine you can produce anything legible with this constant rocking. I am persuaded it cannot be much further."

"I am not writing a letter, Aunt Fanny. I thought we might play Bouts-Rime to pass the time."

"An excellent idea. But I will find it far too fatiguing to think of a suitable rhyme, so if you do not object, I will just listen."

"As you wish." Marianne handed the piece of paper to Georgianna. "You go first, you are always much quicker than I at thinking of a verse."

"Very well." Georgianna looked down at if for a few moments and began to murmur under her breath. "Mind, sorrow, kind, morrow." After a moment she smiled.

"Never should an elegant mind,
Show excess of joy or sorrow,
For neither will prove cruel or kind,
But both be gone upon the morrow."

"Very good, Lady Georgianna," said Miss Bragg. "And very true. I have often thought that to live all in alt must be extremely wearing."

"It is," said Lady Brancaster softly, her gaze drifting to where Sir Robert rode beside the carriage. "It was one of the reasons I chose Lord Brancaster. He kept me on an even keel. As do you, Aurora."

Marianne looked closely at her aunt, but for once, said nothing.

Georgianna took the pencil and put a neat line through Marianne's words. Her brow creased in thought, and then she jotted down a few of her own and passed the paper to Miss Bragg.

"Thank you, Lady Georgianna. I do enjoy word games, I must admit." She frowned down at the elegant writing and then held the paper at arms length. "Oh, I see. Unclear, heart, dear, part." She looked out of the window for a moment as if for inspiration, then nodded decisively.

"*The path ahead may seem unclear,*
The head oft rules the heart,
But hold to things that you hold dear,
And from them never part."

Georgianna held Miss Bragg's eyes for a long moment and then nodded and smiled.

Miss Bragg now took the pencil and regarded Marianne for a moment before adding her own words under Georgianna's. As she passed it to her, Lady Brancaster suddenly exclaimed, "Oh, I think this must be it."

Marianne folded the paper and put it away, leaning forwards slightly to see out of the far window.

The landscape in this part of the country was unusually open, neither marked by hedgerows or woods, but now a high stone wall imposed itself upon the wide vista. Above it the leafy boughs of ancient trees swayed gently in the breeze, some overhanging the obstruction as if trying to escape their confinement.

It was some time before they came to the lodge that signalled the entrance into the park. The difference between the rough parched grasslands outside the walls and the green, fertile landscape within was marked. They drove for some time through the woodland, enjoying the cool, dappled shade.

"I have always wished to see Cranbourne," Lady Brancaster said. "I have heard that it is a very grand house."

Her wish was granted not many moments later. They turned a bend in the road and left the wood behind. Before them spread rolling parklands, divided by a winding river. The land sloped gently upwards on the far side of the water, before levelling out again. Cranbourne sat graciously at the top of the rise. It was built of a mellow, golden stone, and consisted of four three-storey wings set around a courtyard. At the end of each were impressive corner towers, a storey higher. The central façade of the front of the building also rose to four storeys, and set above the huge arched doorway, a wide double-height window glinted in the sunshine.

"It is magnificent," Lady Brancaster breathed. "No wonder all the matchmaking mamas have thrown their daughters at Lord Cranbourne's head. It would be quite something to be mistress of such a grand establishment."

"Indeed it would," agreed Miss Bragg. "There cannot be many finer houses to be found anywhere in the country! And just look at this bridge. I have never seen the like!"

They crossed the river by way of a covered Palladian bridge, the roof supported by tall classical columns, the whole in the style of a Roman temple.

Marianne began to feel a little daunted. Cranbourne was a far cry from her own home. Harwich Court was a sprawling, homely house, whose decor had been chosen for comfort rather than to impress, whereas the building before her was nothing if not imposing.

What had the man who had rescued her from a hovel to do with all this splendour? Lord Cranbourne had always dressed with an understated elegance that she admired, but in her ignorance she had not realised that his attire was probably as expensive as it was simple. No wonder he sometimes assumed what she had called his haughty manner. She blushed now at her temerity. To be raised in such an environment must instil a certain measure of pride in the recipient of such an upbringing. And in all fairness, apart from at their first meeting, perhaps, she could not accuse him of any unreasonable amount of conceit. On the contrary he had shown her party a flattering degree of attention and consideration, culminating in his generous invitation to Cranbourne.

They pulled into the long gravelled sweep in front of the large arched door. The butler, housekeeper, and two footmen awaited them. The footmen rushed forwards to put down the steps and help them alight from the carriage, before one of them climbed up next to the coachman to direct him to the stables.

The butler greeted them with cool politeness. "Welcome to Cranbourne. I am Wilmot and this is Mrs Stevens. Please do not hesitate to let us know if we can do anything to make your stay more comfortable."

"Thank you, Wilmot," Lady Brancaster said, before nodding politely at the housekeeper. "Mrs Stevens."

"I will see you later, ladies," Sir Robert said. "I wish to see what sort of cattle Cranbourne keeps."

"Certainly, sir," Wilmot said. "The footman will show you to your room as soon as you have satisfied your curiosity."

He turned back to Lady Brancaster. "Our visitors have taken a trip into Salisbury to view the cathedral and Lord Cranbourne has been out on the estate since early this morning and has not yet returned. May I suggest that it might be the perfect opportunity for you to see something of the house and get your bearings? Unless you are perhaps too tired after your journey?"

"Not at all, it would do us all good to stretch our legs, I am sure."

Mrs Stevens dipped into a curtsy. "I will bring some refreshments to the green parlour in twenty minutes, ma'am."

They were led through a series of large, lofty rooms, all marked by their grandeur and regal elegance. Everything spoke of opulence and taste. The well-proportioned rooms boasted huge marble fire-places surmounted by gilt framed mirrors, were often scattered with plush velvet chairs and sofas, and most had finely carved mouldings and impressive murals painted on the ceilings. The book-lined library must have been fifty feet long at least, and allowed them a glimpse of the formal gardens that lay beyond. The more natural park in front of the house, had here been ruthlessly sculpted and shaped into parterres, the narrow gravelled walkways all leading to a large, circular fountain.

The wide curving staircase that led to the first floor, was lined with paintings, and Marianne fancifully felt as if the many eyes of the Cranbourne ancestors were coolly assessing her, and most likely finding her unworthy of their scrutiny.

The huge double-height window they had spied from the carriage was mirrored at the far end of the room and allowed light to pour into the long gallery, which was filled with the finest statuary, including a full-length statue of the current earl.

"It is a family tradition," the butler informed them. "Each earl for the last five generations has had his form sculpted. I think you will agree that Lord Cranbourne's likeliness has been caught very well."

Marianne could not disagree, although this was the cool, aloof Lord Cranbourne she had glimpsed across the pump room.

"Indeed it has," Miss Bragg murmured. "There seems to be a remarkable likeness between all the earls. It is in the aquiline nose and firm jaw, I think."

"It is true, of course," Wilmot said. "But if Viscount Woodley, who was the first born son, had not succumbed to the fever which took his father, the case would have been different. He took after Lady Cranbourne in looks and temperament."

At the end of the twenty minutes they were very pleased to sit in the cosy apple green sitting room that had been set aside for their private use during their stay. Mrs Stevens brought in the tea tray herself.

"We dine at six," she informed them. "Everyone generally gathers in the blue saloon from five thirty."

Marianne and Georgianna's rooms were adjacent to each other, with a large dressing room between them. Nancy was unusually flustered by her grand surroundings but determined to ensure both ladies did her credit. After some discussion about their preferred dresses for the evening, which involved much back and forth for the maid, she turned an exasperated glance on Lady Georgianna, who had a very firm vision as to her raiment and her hair arrangement.

"I agree the pale green silk will do nicely. But if you want me to do your hair justice, it would be much easier, Lady Georgianna, if you would come into Miss Montagu's room so I am not running about like a headless chicken."

Georgianna raised no demur. "Of course, Nancy. It is a very sensible suggestion."

She found Marianne slowly pulling a brush through her long dark locks. She was already dressed in a simple round gown of fine Indian muslin trimmed with pink satin.

"See to Georgianna first, Nancy," she murmured absently.

Nancy was very happy to comply with this suggestion as Lady Georgianna, who usually preferred a quite simple, if not severe style, had chosen this of all evenings to request a more sophisticated look.

It took a good twenty minutes to arrange her thick ebony locks. Two thinly woven braids softened the hair that was pulled back from her face before being artfully arranged in a knot surrounded by cascading curls.

"You are very quiet, Marianne," Georgianna said, as Nancy worked her magic.

"I am feeling a little intimidated," she admitted. "I do not know what to expect, or even whom we are to meet."

Georgianna raised a surprised brow. "Marianne, you sound like Charlotte! What is it that daunts you?"

Marianne gave a rueful smile. "I do, don't I? I believe these opulent surroundings have quite sunk my spirits. You know what an unruly tongue I have. I would sink myself beneath reproach if I were to embarrass Aunt Fanny by acting or speaking in an incorrect manner."

Georgianna did not move an inch as Nancy pushed the final pin into her hair, but her considering gaze met her friend's in the mirror.

"Marianne, you are my first real friend and I hold you in high esteem. If you have taught me anything, it is that wealth or family history does not alone raise you above others. Such consequence and conceit is contemptible. Curb your unruly tongue, by all means, but do not be anything but yourself in whatever company we find ourselves. I think the thing that has impressed me most in all our dealings, is your honesty and your strong sense of who you are."

Marianne's eyes widened at such an accolade from her very correct friend.

"She's quite right, miss," Nancy said gruffly. "Your father is a fine man, and if he is proud of you – and I can assure you that he is – why should you worrit about what anyone else will think of you?"

Marianne felt a weight shift from her shoulders. "Thank you, both of you," she said, a smile curving her lips. "I shall look upon this then, as another splendid adventure to be enjoyed."

Nancy removed the brush from her fingers and briskly brushed out the last of her tangles. "You do that, miss. But if you get any more madcap ideas in your head, make sure you run them past Lady Georgianna or Lady Brancaster before you put them into action."

The maid only had time to twist Marianne's hair into a simple knot before Lady Brancaster and Miss Bragg appeared.

"Good, you are ready. Come along now, girls, it has turned half past five already and I do hate to be the last to arrive at any gathering."

She hurried them down several corridors and two flights of stairs. The door to the blue saloon was ajar and as they approached the exasperated tones of Lord Cranbourne reached them with disastrous clarity.

"It is the outside of enough, Maria. How could you be so rag mannered to have not been present to greet our guests?"

"Must I remind you, Anthony, that they are *your* guests? And you were not here either, were you?"

"That will not fadge, sister. I have many responsibilities to attend to at Cranbourne, as well you know. You have only one. To be the hostess of this damned house party."

"I would ask you to mind your language, brother—"

Lady Brancaster had heard enough. Putting a finger to her lips she tiptoed back up the corridor a short way and then gave a tinkling laugh. "You were right, Lady Georgianna. It is this way. I vow, left to my own devices I would get hopelessly lost."

The voices abruptly stopped and by the time they entered the room, Lady Strickland was seated demurely by the fireplace, and Lord Cranbourne was standing casually in front of it, any look of vexation erased from his brow.

He came forwards and bowed. "Welcome to Cranbourne. Lady Georgianna, Miss Montagu, please let me introduce my sister, Lady Strickland."

That lady had also inherited the firm chin and aquiline nose of the family. She bowed her head regally and regarded the two young ladies of the party closely for a moment before turning to Lady Brancaster.

"I am glad to see you have finally entered society again, Lady Brancaster. It seems an age since I last saw you."

"Thank you for your warm welcome, Lady Strickland. Please accept my apologies for descending on you with such short notice. I know how much extra work it must have made for you."

Lady Strickland visibly thawed. "Oh, do not apologise, Lady Brancaster. It is hardly your fault." She glanced at Lord Cranbourne. "Brothers can be such inconsiderate creatures, can't they?"

Lady Brancaster gave another tinkling laugh. "I shall have to take your word for it, not having any myself, you understand. I do have a brother-in-law, if that counts? But I must say he has the most amiable disposition."

"Then you are very fortunate, ma'am," she said shortly. Her eyes skimmed over Marianne and came to rest on Lady Georgianna.

"You have your mama's eyes." She gestured to the blue velvet sofa behind her. "Come, sit with me, Lady Georgianna. It is such a pity your mother so rarely visits town these days, I do so enjoy her company. You must tell me what she has been up to."

Marianne glanced down at Miss Bragg who correctly interpreted the relieved look in her eyes.

"Being invisible sometimes has its advantages," she murmured.

Marianne smiled, but glanced up as Sir Robert followed four others into the room. Even before Lord Cranbourne introduced them, she realised that they must be the Ponsonbys, for the young lady was just as Sir Horace had described. Her blue eyes, pale, flawless complexion and flaxen hair did indeed remind her of a china doll. The young man beside her could only be her brother, for he bore a striking resemblance to her. He should have been handsome, she thought, but his chin was a little weak and his slenderness gave him a delicate appearance.

"Tell me, Miss Montagu," Miss Ponsonby said, "what do you make of Cranbourne? Is it not divine?"

Lord Cranbourne stood close by them talking to Lord and Lady Ponsonby, but on hearing the question put to Miss Montagu, he turned to her and quirked an enquiring brow, a glimmer of a challenge in his eyes.

She raised her chin a little, but picked her words with care. "I am barely acquainted with it as yet and so it would be premature of me to form any judgement, in case I do not do it justice."

She winced slightly, as Miss Ponsonby gave an extraordinarily high-pitched trill of laughter.

"Oh, you must be funning, Miss Montagu. I am sure I had barely taken a step over the threshold before I realised how fortunate I was to be in such splendid surroundings."

"I am glad you find Cranbourne to your liking, Miss Ponsonby," Lord Cranbourne said. His gaze again turned to Marianne, his eyes enigmatic. "I will look forward to hearing your considered opinion in a few days, Miss Montagu. I am sure it will be most enlightening."

He suddenly stiffened, his countenance becoming as cold and aloof as the likeness of him sculpted in marble. Marianne's heart sank as she wondered if she had insulted him, but then she realised he was looking over her head. Turning, she saw that a lady, who was almost of a height with Georgianna, had entered the room. Her hair was more golden than blonde, and she was breathtakingly beautiful. Her celestial blue dress was vary daring, and clung to her slender yet curvaceous form.

As soon as this lady's eyes met Lord Cranbourne's, she withdrew her arm from the slightly stooped, grey haired gentleman beside her, and ignoring everyone else in the room, advanced unhurriedly, her softly rounded hips swaying with each step she took. She came to a halt in front of him and rested her closed fan against her lips. After a moment, she drew it gently across her cheek.

"I think it quite unworthy of you to treat such old friends in so cavalier a fashion, Lord Cranbourne. Was your business really so very pressing that you could not have joined us on our expedition?"

"Ah, but I have seen the cathedral many times, Lady Silchester, and going over old ground can become so tedious," he said softly.

"Oh, how can you say so?" protested Lady Ponsonby. "I declare, the cathedral is so architecturally beautiful, I could visit it a thousand times and never be disappointed."

Lord Cranbourne's eyes never left Lady Silchester's as he replied, "Yes, but it is a cold sort of beauty. It lacks heart, I think."

Marianne saw a flash of annoyance light Lady Silchester's eyes. The tension between the two was palpable.

Lady Strickland hastily bustled forwards as two more people arrived, her sharp voice knifing through the heavy silence that had suddenly fallen upon the room. "There you are, Strickland. Wherever have you been?"

"Well, my dear——"

She held up an imperious hand. "No, do not tell me. I am sure you and Lord Wedmore have been sharing sporting tales of derring-do that cannot be of the least interest to the ladies. Besides, it is high time we went into dinner."

CHAPTER 13

The thought that neither of the slightly portly gentlemen before her seemed the sort to perform any acts of derring-do, sporting or otherwise, crossed Marianne's mind before the import of Lady Strickland's words hit home.

Lord Wedmore! Her eyes flew to where she had last seen Georgianna in conversation with Lady Strickland. She stood like a statue, her back ramrod straight, her bearing proud, and her eyes providing the only splash of colour in her white face. She hurriedly crossed to her side and curled her arm through hers.

"Is it not the most outrageous coincidence that he should be here?" Marianne whispered.

The touch of her friend seemed to breathe life back into Georgianna. Her bloodless lips twisted into an ironic smile. Marianne was surprised to see a glitter of cold humour in the eyes that looked down at her. "Indeed. If I was not aware of the fact that Lady Brancaster's letter, informing my mother of our change of plans could only just have reached her, I would suspect her of engineering the whole."

As the party was large and of an odd number, Marianne found herself seated in the middle of the table between Lady Georgianna and Mr Ponsonby. She was pleased that Lord Silchester took the chair on the other side of her friend, the honour of sitting next to Lord Wedmore – who was thankfully placed on the other side of the table – falling to Miss Ponsonby.

As her brother seemed frequently tongue-tied, spending most of his time pushing the food around his plate in a rather moody manner, and Lord Silchester frequently engaged Georgianna in gentle conversation, she was left plenty of leisure to covertly observe the various interactions of the other members of the party.

She was pleased to see that Lady Ponsonby, although a viscountess, was quite happy to bestow upon Miss Bragg a flattering degree of attention. Indeed, she was very grateful that this was the case, for she had a fondness for her aunt's companion, and Sir Robert, who sat on her other side, was quite taken up with Lady Silchester. He really did not have much choice, as that lady was pointedly ignoring Lord Cranbourne.

If Marianne had wished for a lesson in flirting, she was certainly now receiving it. Even without hearing their hushed conversation, she could not fail to interpret the coquettish glances Lady Silchester cast in Sir Robert's direction from beneath her long, curling lashes. Neither did Marianne miss her habit, of every now and then, laying a hand upon his arm, or the way she occasionally turned and leaned towards him as if to catch his words, offering him a glimpse of her ample cleavage.

Marianne cast more than one anxious sideways glance at her aunt, but was relieved to see that her eyes did not once flicker in their direction. She was dividing her attention very politely between Lord Cranbourne and Lord Ponsonby.

Her gaze drifted more than once in the direction of Lord Wedmore as she endeavoured to form her own opinion of him. She could not help but think that Georgianna's description of him had been a little exaggerated. She would be surprised if he proved to be any older than her aunt, and to call him fat, she felt an injustice. Aunt Fanny had described him as preachy and prosy – and he certainly seemed to do most of the talking – but Miss Ponsonby did not look at all bored. On the contrary, she listened to him intently, only occasionally interrupting his monologue with a comment of her own. He seemed most gratified by this attention, and regarded her with a benevolent eye.

She would have liked to discuss her observations with Lady Georgianna when the ladies withdrew to the drawing room but did not get the chance, as Lady Silchester seemed intent on furthering an acquaintance with her.

"Let us stroll around the room together, Lady Georgianna. It is so rare that I find another lady of a similar stature to myself. It is so uncomfortable to be always bending down to catch the words of one smaller than oneself, don't you think?"

The older ladies gathered together and were soon engrossed in conversations about a host of people

Marianne had never heard of, leaving her to engage with Miss Ponsonby.

"Are you enjoying your stay?" she enquired politely.

To her surprise, Miss Ponsonby sent a rather furtive glance in the direction of her mother. Seeing that she was hanging upon the words of Lady Strickland, she said, "Of course. Although…"

Marianne leaned a little closer and said encouragingly, "Although?"

The rather brittle gaiety that had marked their earlier interactions abruptly deserted her.

"I do not know why, Miss Montagu, but I feel I can confide in you. Am I right? Can I trust you?"

Marianne looked into her wide eyes and saw vulnerability and fear. She smiled kindly at her and stood, offering her arm. "Come, let us also take a turn about the room."

They passed Lady Silchester and Lady Georgianna coming in the other direction and exchanged polite nods. When they were out of earshot, Miss Ponsonby said, "I admired you greatly earlier, when you did not immediately go into raptures over Cranbourne."

Marianne's brows shot up. "But you expressed such admiration for it."

Miss Ponsonby nodded and said confidingly, "I know. But I was only repeating the words Mama has been drumming into me ever since we were invited. In truth, I find it all rather overwhelming."

Marianne smiled gently at her. "I understand completely, Miss Ponsonby. My home is far more humble, I assure you."

"I somehow knew you would understand. I was so relieved when I heard Lord Cranbourne was not able to attend, although Mama was cross as crabs."

"Why so?"

"Because during the season, she was forever pushing me in his path. She was determined that I would be the one to finally catch him." Her face fell. "Which is completely ridiculous, for I feel so very nervous in his company that I always say something completely nonsensical."

"You do not wish to engage him?" Marianne said, surprised.

"Oh, no. I always do and say precisely what Mama has instructed me to, but he looks at me in a way that makes me feel terribly uncomfortable."

"He has been rude to you?"

"Not at all." Her brow wrinkled in thought. "I find it very hard to explain. If anything, he is meticulously polite. But so distant, so cold."

"And you have informed your mama of this?"

"Oh yes. But she just scolds me and says that it is not important. She is on very good terms with Lady Strickland, and between them they seem to feel that I might do for him. But I won't, I am sure of it."

"Smile," Marianne whispered, as they approached the others and she noticed Lady Ponsonby's eyes upon them. She suddenly laughed. "Yes, I quite agree. You are very right, Miss Ponsonby. Pea green does not suit me either, it makes me look quite ill."

When they had turned about again, she murmured, "Perhaps you should just be yourself, Miss Ponsonby. How is any gentleman to form an opinion of your true character if you only speak your mother's words? I could not help but notice that you seemed quite comfortable in Lord Wedmore's company at dinner."

"Oh, yes. I found him very agreeable, I assure you. Although I must admit that he talked about things of which I know very little. He did not treat my ignorance with contempt, however, but took the time to explain them to me."

"What sort of things?"

Miss Ponsonby's face became quite animated. "Well, apparently not far from here, there is a very ancient circle of stones. Many stories have been told of their origin and purpose. Some have said it is a Roman temple to Apollo, others that it was raised by Merlin, who was magician to King Arthur, and that it is the burial place of kings, although it is now widely believed to be a druid temple. To be honest, I am still not very clear what druids are, but it sounds terribly romantic, don't you think?"

"I must say it does sound very intriguing," admitted Marianne.

They were just passing the door when it opened and Lord Cranbourne came into the room. Miss Ponsonby blushed and hurried away.

He glanced at Marianne and gave a wry smile. "Should my ears be burning, Miss Montagu?"

He looked ridiculously attractive when his eyes glinted with amusement. Her lips quirked in response, and she bit her lip to hold back the almost overpowering urge to tell him how conceited he sounded.

"Not as far as I am aware."

His grin widened and she felt a flutter in her stomach. "How very restrained, Miss Montagu. But you do not deceive me for an instant. You are itching to tell me how puffed up in my own importance I am."

A gurgle of laughter escaped her. "Well you did sound it, but I do not really believe that you are."

He gave her a mock bow. "I am humbled by your good opinion, ma'am."

"I do not believe that either." She smiled. "I am sure you must have some good qualities, but humble is not one of them, I think."

He laughed. "You damn me with faint praise, Miss Montagu. I am sure everyone must have some good qualities. Come, tell me, what are mine?"

"Now you do sound conceited. I will have to know you better before I can comment."

His eyes deepened to that smoky shade she had seen once before. "Then I look forward to you knowing me better," he said softly.

She felt the heat rise to her cheeks and took half a step backwards. "I suppose that is inevitable as I am staying in your house, sir."

"Ah, Cranbourne," Lady Strickland said. "If you gentlemen are ready to join us, I will have some card tables set up."

Marianne watched his cold mask slip into place. He turned to his sister. "Please do, if you ladies would like to play. But I have come to tell you that we gentlemen will not be joining you this evening. We are playing a billiards tournament."

Lady Strickland's bosom swelled. "Well, really! You might have mentioned this to me earlier, Cranbourne. I have had no time to prepare any other amusements for our guests."

"I could not inform you earlier, ma'am, as it has only just been decided."

"Well, do not worry on my account." Lady Brancaster said, rising to her feet. "I for one, feel quite fatigued after today's journey and so shall retire." Her glance rested on her charges. "Girls, I am sure that you also must be a little tired."

Marianne and Lady Georgianna dutifully followed her and Miss Bragg from the room. "Come to my chamber when you are ready for bed," Marianne whispered. "I would be very interested to hear your observations on the evening."

"How do you find things here, Nancy?" she asked as her maid helped her out of her gown. "Have you been treated well?"

"Yes, miss," she said. "In all truth, I was expecting the servants here to be a little starched up, but that has not been the case at all. They have been dignified, as you might expect, but very helpful."

"I am glad."

"Don't you go worriting about me, miss. I can look after myself. Now, I must see to Lady Georgianna, so you just climb into that huge bed and get some rest."

She sat with her knees curled up before her whilst she waited for Georgianna, her mind playing over the various scenes she had witnessed. Her thoughts were repeatedly drawn back to Lord Cranbourne. She still found him very difficult to fathom. She did not think that coldness was his natural habit. When he had cut her bonds in the farmhouse, his eyes had flashed with anger at her treatment. And when he teased her, she saw warmth and humour in his eyes. Yet she could understand Miss Ponsonby's feelings. If he had treated her with the same cold politeness he dealt to Lady Strickland, it was hardly surprising she wanted none of him.

And then there was his treatment of Lady Silchester. Although his words to her had been softly spoken, there had been ice in every one of them. What had happened between them for him to talk to her so?

She gave a start as Georgianna sat on the edge of the bed.

"I did not mean to startle you," she said softly. "Whatever were you thinking of? You looked very serious."

"Climb under the covers. It has turned quite cold."

Georgianna's brows rose but she slipped under the blankets. "Do you not wear a cap for bed?"

"No, I find it much more comfortable without one. Although I often regret it when Nancy attacks my tangles in the morning. Tell me, how did you find Lady Silchester?"

"Inquisitive," Georgianna said dryly. "She was very interested in how we came to meet Lord Cranbourne. She also took it upon herself to proffer me some advice."

Marianne rolled onto her side, the better to observe her friend. "Go on," she urged.

A cold little smile played around the edges of Georgianna's mouth. "She told me a tale which I fancy is partly true and partly fuelled by her own desires." She glanced at Marianne's wide eyes and mimicked Lady Silchester's clear, superior tones to perfection. "You seem to me a very well bred girl,

Lady Georgianna. But you are still just a girl, after all. Might I just drop a gentle word of warning in your ear? You are just the type to catch Lord Cranbourne's eye, but I am afraid that is all you are likely to catch. His heart, I am sad to say, has been lost for many years."

"To whom?" breathed Marianne.

"Patience, impetuous one." Lady Georgianna assumed a rueful expression "To me, I am afraid. He was madly in love with me when I was not much older than you. He proposed to me, of course, but how could I accept when he had no title or the prospect of one at that time? My parents would never have countenanced the match. He has never looked at another woman in the same way ever since and has now acquired the reputation of trifling with the affections of more than one lady, but it never comes to anything. I would not like you to raise your hopes only to have them dashed in so cruel a manner. You heard how cuttingly he spoke to me earlier, he has still not forgiven me."

"So that's it." Marianne's brow wrinkled. "But why did she think he might trifle with you?"

"Because, my innocent friend, Lady Silchester still thinks in terms of rank. She married Lord Silchester because she wished to become a marchioness, and I am the highest ranking young lady at this house party."

"Oh, I see," Marianne murmured.

"But I do not believe he is still languishing after her. I think you will find it is the other way around."

"Why do you say so?"

"Because Lord Silchester, who I found to be a very

interesting and entertaining gentleman, is getting old and infirm. Imagine the irony of the situation. She married the marquis not long before the Earl of Cranbourne and his heir died. She could have been the Countess of Cranbourne if she had perhaps followed her heart, but she is not, and I do not think she wishes anyone else to be either."

"Well it serves her right," muttered Marianne. "I do not believe she has a heart. Did you not see how outrageously she flirted with Sir Robert this evening?"

"I did. I think she was trying to make Lord Cranbourne jealous. But again her calculations misfired. It was she who was made jealous, when he stood smiling and laughing with you."

Marianne considered her exchange with Lord Cranbourne. "Perhaps that was his intention."

"I doubt it." Georgianna yawned. "He has always enjoyed your company. How did you find Miss Ponsonby?"

"She is a sweet ninny hammer," Marianne said. "Her mother hopes she will become the next countess, but she does not like Lord Cranbourne." She gave her friend a mischievous look. "She seemed much more taken with Lord Wedmore. If you can discourage him enough, Georgianna, it may be that he might reconsider who he wishes to marry."

Georgianna's lashes fluttered closed as she murmured, "I shall do my very best, of that you can be sure."

When Nancy came to blow out the candles not many minutes later, she found them both fast asleep.

CHAPTER 14

The gentlemen enjoyed quite a lively evening, their competitive instinct undimmed regardless of their age or the quantity of wine they had consumed. Only Lord Silchester and Mr Ponsonby did not play. The former kept track of the score as he could no longer bend over the table without a considerable degree of discomfort.

"Mind you, I could have beaten you all hollow not very many moons ago," he assured them with a twinkle.

Mr Ponsonby, much to his father's disgust, preferred to sit in the window seat, gazing dreamily out at the moonlit garden.

"Come, boy. It is time you joined in with manly pursuits. You cannot spend your life in a daydream."

"Leave him," Lord Cranbourne said gently. "There are enough of us to make the tournament interesting."

But with each glass of wine Lord Ponsonby drank, the more his exasperated glance rested on his progeny until he finally snapped, "Oh, get yourself to bed, boy. You are an embarrassment."

Colouring, Mr Ponsonby rose to his feet, bowed, and hurriedly left the room, closing the door none too gently behind him.

"You are too hard on him," Lord Silchester said softly. "We are not all cut from the same cloth, after all."

"So it would seem." Lord Ponsonby scowled. "If I didn't know my good lady was everything that is loyal and virtuous, I would suspect he was not cut from my cloth at all! Fancies himself an artist!"

"And is he any good?" Lord Silchester asked, interested.

"Lord, how would I know? And what if he is? Ponsonby Hall is as full of paintings as it can hold. He needs his feet on the ground if he is to run the estate after I am gone, not his head in the clouds."

"And do the two activities need to be mutually exclusive?"

Lord Ponsonby took another gulp of wine and regarded the older gentleman with some hostility. "Come, man. You have two young sons of your own. Do not tell me that you won't have something to say if your eldest does not square up to his responsibilities when the time comes!"

Lord Silchester smiled gently. "If I am so fortunate to live long enough to see my sons reach maturity, you may be sure I shall not insist they put duty ahead of their happiness. It would only breed resentment, and their estates would become a gilded cage from which they longed to escape. I think you will find that a good steward is better than a reluctant landlord."

"At least you have nothing to blush for in your daughter," Lord Wedmore said. "She has very pretty manners."

Lord Ponsonby looked a little mollified. "I am glad that you think so, sir."

"You've got me again, damn you, Cranbourne." Lord Strickland shook his victor's hand with good grace. "But I don't mind losing to such a fine fellow. This was a damn fine idea of yours, haven't enjoyed myself half so much since I arrived!" His eyes suddenly widened as he realised his comment might not be very complimentary to the other guests present. "I don't mean to say, it's not that I—"

Lord Silchester took pity on him and with a satirical smile, interrupted his stammerings. "I am sure we all understand you, Strickland." He glanced down at the scrap of paper in his hand. "Very good, Cranbourne. You remain unbeaten and are the undoubted winner of the tournament. Lord Wedmore and Sir Robert are tied in second place. Now, if you do not mind, I shall retire. I am suddenly feeling a little fatigued."

Lord Wedmore and Sir Robert insisted on the best of three frames to decide who was runner up. Lord Cranbourne was happy that Sir Robert claimed that honour after only two for the evening had begun to pall.

Sir Robert strolled with him towards their bedchambers. "I would be very grateful, old fellow, if you could keep that maneater out from under my feet. If I am not much mistaken, she has done my cause no good this night."

"Then you should not encourage her," Lord Cranbourne said, a trifle shortly.

"I assure you, Cranbourne, that she needed no encouragement. But I am not so ramshackle as to be rude to a guest at your table."

They had reached Lord Cranbourne's room. He paused with his hand on the door handle.

"You need have no qualms on my account, Sir Robert. You must dampen her pretensions. I have no doubt you are quite capable of it. I bid you goodnight."

Although he was tired, sleep was slow in coming. He was furious with Maria for inviting the Silchesters. Her excuse that Lady Silchester had practically invited herself when she had heard of the house party was most likely true, and the prospect of having such high-ranking guests would certainly have been too irresistible for his sister to refuse, even so, he wished that she had done so.

He had no axe to grind with Lord Silchester; he liked him. He looked on the world with a satirical but humorous eye that was very entertaining, but Melissa was another matter. He found it hard now to believe that he had thought himself in love with her. Over the years, the scales had fallen from his eyes and he had seen that she was both calculating and predatory.

The manner in which she flirted so openly with other men in front of her husband was contemptible. If she had shown a little more discretion, he would have felt more kindly towards her, but her coquettish mannerisms were more in the style of a courtesan than a woman of quality. He would certainly not add to Lord Silchester's humiliation by gratifying her vain desires.

Miss Montagu's refreshingly frank, open manners were far more appealing than Melissa's unsubtle lures. But be that as it may, he regretted now his impulsive decision to invite Lady Brancaster and her party, for having done so, it would be unconscionably rude of him to absent himself from whatever entertainments Maria had in store.

He must be careful, however, as much as he enjoyed Miss Montagu's company, he must not raise false hopes in her breast. He suddenly laughed. He did sound like a coxcomb. She had given him no indication that she harboured any desire to become the next Countess of Cranbourne. On the contrary, she had been very cautious in her response to the house and he had certainly felt her withdraw when he had gently flirted with her. Perhaps her lack of ambition was part of her attraction.

He rolled over and sighed. Perhaps it was his own heart that he must guard. Although he knew it was time Cranbourne had a mistress, Miss Montagu was far too young to take on the many and varied responsibilities that would come with the title. How could she look after his many staff and tenants, when she could not even look after herself?

～

When Marianne awoke, Georgianna had gone. She must have woken sometime in the night and tiptoed back to her own room. She grinned as she imagined the surprise her friend must have felt at finding herself asleep in her bed.

When she said as much to Nancy, her maid smiled. "You were both sleeping like babies and I didn't have the heart to wake her. Besides, if you were staying in a smaller house, it would be quite usual to find yourselves thrown in together."

"I would not mind that at all but it would not be fair on Georgianna, I always wake so early."

"That's true enough, miss. Lady Georgianna is still fast asleep."

"I think I will go for a walk in the gardens before breakfast, Nancy. There can be no harm in that, surely?"

"I shouldn't think so, but you'd best put your boots on, miss, it rained quite heavily in the night."

It appeared that Marianne was the first up. A sleepy footman showed her to a side door.

"If you go through the formal garden and across the park a little way, ma'am, you'll find a nice little temple that looks out over the river."

Marianne smiled her thanks. The sun was not very high in the sky as yet, and the tall hedges that marked the boundaries of the formal garden threw it into shadow. Pulling her cloak a little closer around her, she hurried towards the archway on the far side. She passed under it and then paused, breathing deep the fresh morning air. The dew sparkled on the well-kept lawns that sloped gently down towards the river. It glinted invitingly in the morning sunlight. She slowed, treading carefully lest she lose her footing on the slippery grass.

It was not until she could hear the gentle

murmuring of the water that she saw the cream dome of the temple, nestled amongst the trees that lined the far side of its bank. She crossed an elegantly curving stone bridge, noticing that the water ran quite quickly here, swollen by the night's rainfall no doubt.

She approached the temple from the side, and ran up the shallow steps to the tall slender columns that supported it. She halted abruptly as she saw it was not empty. Mr Ponsonby sat in front of an easel, his eyes fixed on the view before him. He was unaware of her presence, and somehow feeling that she was intruding, she cast a quick glance around the temple, noting the impressively carved statue of Apollo set in a niche in the wall, before slowly backing away.

But even as her foot searched for the first step, her cloak billowed in the breeze and he quickly turned his head. His eyes flashed with annoyance and he threw down his brush and dropped his head into his hands.

"Is there no peace to be found anywhere?" he cried.

Marianne froze. There was real anguish in his words. Her instinct was to flee, but she could not ignore his distress. In a moment she recovered, and cautiously approached him.

"Mr Ponsonby, I am sorry to disturb you. I did not think anyone else was yet up. I would not have come in if I had seen you…"

Her words trailed off as her eyes roamed over the canvas he had been working on. He had caught the movement of the river to perfection, and the dappled light on the leaves of the trees was so delicately rendered, she could almost imagine she could hear them rustle in the breeze. Although he had not yet finished the house in the distance, he had already encapsulated its grandeur and majesty. It could be none other than Cranbourne.

"Mr Ponsonby," she breathed. "Your painting is exceptional. It is not just that you have depicted your subject so accurately, it is almost as if you have captured the light and sprinkled it onto your canvas."

He slowly raised his head and looked at her cautiously. "You really think so?"

She was amazed to see such uncertainty in his eyes. How could he doubt it? She smiled at him and said, "Yes, I really think so. My mother loved to paint and I thought that she was very good, but you have a very special talent."

His eyes lit up. "Do you paint, Miss Montagu?"

"I am afraid I have no talent at all, Mr Ponsonby."

His face fell.

"But that does not mean I cannot judge when somebody else has," Marianne assured him. "I suggest you show your painting to Lord Cranbourne when it is finished. I would not be at all surprised if he offered to purchase it. Now, I will leave you in peace."

He suddenly surged to his feet and she was surprised to see him blush.

"I am sorry I was so rude, Miss Montagu. My father does not like me to paint. I had hoped he would leave me at home but he would not countenance it. That is why I sneak off as soon as the sun rises. I have to, you see. If I cannot paint, I feel quite desperate. As if life is not worth living."

The fanatical light in his eyes, made her take a step backwards. "Calm yourself, Mr Ponsonby. What you need is a sponsor. If your father sees that other people admire your work, perhaps he will too. Finish your painting, and then show it to Lord Cranbourne."

He pushed his hands through his limp locks. "Perhaps you are right, Miss Montagu. I have been reluctant to put my work under the scrutiny of others, frightened that they might dismiss it as uninteresting, mundane, or not well executed." He turned and regarded his canvas for a moment, and then murmured, "But I shall, I shall!"

He sat back at his easel and picked up his brush. Marianne knew that she was already forgotten, and turned and ran lightly down the steps. She walked briskly back over the bridge and up to the house, eager to put some distance between herself and Mr Ponsonby. She pitied his uncertainty and his plight, but his emotions had veered in an abrupt manner that had alarmed her.

As she reached the first landing, she paused as she heard someone sobbing. She followed the sound down a long corridor and as she turned a corner was bowled over by a maid running in the opposite direction. They fell to the floor in a tangle of limbs.

"Oh, miss, I am that sorry," the girl gasped.

Marianne sat up and looked into the tear-stained face of the maid. She judged that she was younger than herself, and a bright red mark marred the side of her pale cheek.

"Oh, you poor thing," Marianne said, brushing her fingertips across it. "Did you bang your head when you fell?"

The unlooked for sympathy sent the maid into another flood of tears. "N-no ma'am. I carried up Lady Silchester's hot w-water, and as I put the heavy basin down, some of it scalded me and I went stumbling backwards and knocked into her toilet table. One of her delicate bottles of scent fell off and smashed. She was that angry, she gave me a slap, and I'm sure it's no more than I deserved. I just hope Mrs Stevens don't turn me off. I've only been apprenticed here for a few weeks."

"Apprenticed?" Marianne said.

The maid nodded and swiped her hand across her face. "Yes, ma'am. I'm one of Lord Cranbourne's girls."

Marianne's brows shot up even as her heart sank. "Lord Cranbourne is your father?"

The girl looked at her in astonishment and then despite her worries, gave a watery chuckle. "I might wish that I were, miss, but it is no such thing. I'm one of his orphans."

The maid scrambled to her feet. "I'd best be goin' now, miss, before Mrs Stevens comes lookin' for me. I'm in enough trouble as it is."

"I will come with you," Marianne said. "It may be that I can make things easier for you with Mrs Stevens."

Marianne had gradually taken over her mother's duties at Harwich Court. Their housekeeper had shown her the ropes, and by the time she was fifteen, she was managing things herself. She had thought nothing of going down to the housekeeper's room or the kitchens. Indeed, she had enjoyed learning from cook how to dress a joint or make a cake.

As the maid led her down the backstairs, she said, "Tell me about Lord Cranbourne's orphans."

"There's not much to tell, miss. Lord Cranbourne

and his mother set up an asylum for orphaned girls about five years back. We are given some lessons in reading, writing, and the Bible. We learn how to mend, sew, clean, and cook and when we reach fifteen we are apprenticed out to a family."

They turned into the corridor that led to the kitchens.

"There you are, Martha. What kept you? There is more water going cold—"

Mrs Stevens looked at Marianne in some astonishment. "Miss Montagu, how can I help you? You had only to send your maid or ring the bell if you required anything."

As Martha flew into the kitchen, Marianne smiled sweetly at the housekeeper. "Might I have a word, Mrs Stevens, in private?"

"Of course, ma'am. Please come into my sitting room."

By the end of ten minutes both ladies found they were equally pleased with the other. Mrs Stevens was touched by Marianne's thoughtfulness and pleased with her practical, down-to-earth attitude. In turn, Marianne was impressed by the housekeeper's good sense and reasonable view of the situation.

"They always take a little while to settle in," Mrs Stevens said. "They teach them very well up at the asylum, but of course they don't have to deal with the quality there, and it always makes them nervous at first."

As Marianne was not very sure of her way from the kitchens, she retraced her and Martha's steps. As she stepped back onto the main landing, she surprised

Lord Cranbourne who had just returned from his early morning ride.

"Miss Montagu! Whatever are you doing using the servants' stairs?"

She watched him stride down the corridor towards her, and felt a blush stain her cheeks as he came to a halt in front of her.

"Lord Cranbourne. I owe you an apology."

His brows winged up. "Whatever for?"

"If you remember, sir, when we were at Cheltenham, I said something about it being every gentleman's responsibility to think of those less fortunate than themselves. And now I find you have an asylum for orphaned young girls."

His dark brows snapped together. "How the deuce did you find out?"

Marianne was surprised by his annoyed response. "What does that matter?" she replied, her voice cool. "I wronged you and I am sorry. Now, if you will excuse me, I must go and tidy myself up before breakfast."

She hurried back to her room, surprised to feel the sharp sting of tears in her eyes. Her apology had been sincere. Why should he not want her to know of his generosity? She was as far from understanding him as ever. But one thing of which she was certain was that she had had quite enough of mercurial temperaments this morning. She would take breakfast in her room and then write the long overdue letter to her stepmother. She was beginning to understand how easy it was to be misunderstood. And how painful.

CHAPTER 15

L ord Cranbourne stood frowning at her hastily retreating back for a moment, and then took the backstairs himself, two at a time. Had he been mistaken in her? Was she as duplicitous as so many others of her sex? Did she present that open frank exterior to the world, and then go snooping around asking the servants questions? He hoped not. For if he found any of his had been gossiping about him, they would soon regret it.

A few minutes conversation with Mrs Stevens was enough to make him feel like a cad.

"She is a very nice young lady, sir. She would have been more than justified in haranguing Martha for knocking her down. But she just laughed it off. She was much more concerned that she did not get into any trouble. I'm sure Lady Silchester had every right to slap her – the bottle of scent she broke probably cost a fortune – but Miss Montagu did not quite see it that way. She felt very sorry for the girl."

He returned hurriedly to his room to wash and change for breakfast. He must apologise to Miss Montagu. Although how he would explain his strange reaction to her words was not entirely clear to him. He would hardly cast himself in a good light if he admitted he had suspected her of interrogating his servants.

He felt even more of a brute when she did not come down for breakfast. Her absence was not remarked on, indeed a few others had also decided to take it in their room and he was glad to note that Lady Silchester was among them.

He glanced down the table at his guests and suppressed an ironic smile. Perhaps it was better that Miss Montagu had not come down, for he was sure she would have dealt him the same treatment Sir Robert was receiving from Lady Brancaster. He had seated himself beside her but she seemed fascinated by Lord Silchester and paid him no heed. Lord Wedmore sat between Lady Georgianna and Miss Ponsonby, and as the former responded to him in a very haughty manner whenever he addressed her, it was only natural that he turn to the latter, who smiled shyly up at him and seemed to hang on his every word. This was not the Miss Ponsonby he had encountered in town, indeed, it was a vast improvement.

He was not surprised that Lord Strickland had not joined them, let off his sister's very short leash, he had hit the bottle quite heavily last night, and whilst not being drunk as a wheelbarrow, he had certainly been a trifle disguised. Even as these thoughts flitted across his mind, Maria entered the breakfast parlour.

She cast a quick glance about the room and came and sat by him.

"Good morning, Cranbourne," she said, her mouth pursed. "I hope you enjoyed yourself last evening?"

"Thank you, Maria. It was reasonably successful, I think."

"I am glad to hear it. But as you deserted us ladies last evening, might I request that you do not disappear off fishing or some such thing today?"

"What have you got in mind?" he asked cautiously.

"I thought we might set out a game of quoits on the lawn, and perhaps have a nuncheon down by the river later."

"If you don't mind me interrupting, ma'am," Lord Wedmore said. "Miss Ponsonby is very interested in the circle of standing stones that are not too far from here, I believe."

"You are?" Lady Strickland said, regarding her with some surprise. "I had not realised you were so interested in ancient history, Miss Ponsonby."

"I am not as a rule," she admitted. "But Lord Wedmore has made the stones sound very intriguing. Miss Montagu thought so too when I told her the stories about them."

"If you wish to visit Stonehenge, you shall, Miss Ponsonby," Lord Cranbourne said decisively. "It is less than an hour away by carriage and we can enjoy a nuncheon as much there as anywhere else."

For once, Lady Strickland did not complain about the abrupt change to her carefully laid plans, pleased that he had acceded so readily to Miss Ponsonby's wishes.

A variety of carriages cluttered the gravelled sweep in front of the house less than two hours later. The guests gathered on the lawn and Lord Wedmore took it upon himself to regale them with the various stories that had been woven over time about the mysterious place.

Lady Silchester yawned and turned to Lady Brancaster who stood beside her. "That man is such a bore," she murmured.

Lady Brancaster merely raised a brow.

Lady Silchester's eyes brightened as Lord Cranbourne and Sir Robert suddenly appeared, driving their curricles at a smart pace around the corner of the house. They pulled up and jumped nimbly down. Lord Cranbourne strode briskly towards his guests and she smiled widely at him, fanning herself languidly.

"Perhaps you might take me up—"

Her fan snapped shut as he did not appear to hear her, but strode straight past and bowed to Miss Montagu. "I hear you have an interest in the stones, Miss Montagu. If you would allow me to drive you, I will be happy to answer any questions you may have as best I can."

Her eyes widened and she turned to Miss Bragg as if for support.

"Off you go, dear," she said. "It is always interesting to be guided by someone who knows the locality so intimately."

Sir Robert paused by Lady Silchester to let them pass.

She opened her eyes very wide. "Sir Robert, I do so hate to be crushed in a barouche, might there be room for me to ride with you?"

Lady Brancaster stiffened as he bowed before her.

"I am sorry to disappoint you, Lady Silchester, but that place has already been reserved for another."

He looked at Lady Brancaster and offered his arm. After a moment, she smiled and allowed him to escort her to his curricle.

"Come, dearest," said Lord Silchester approaching his wife. "You will be far more comfortable in the barouche. You may draw up the hood to keep the sun off your delicate complexion. You know how much you suffer in the heat and it would not do for the brightest diamond here to lose her lustre."

She laughed brightly. "You are right, of course, my lord. I had forgotten, how silly of me."

A rather awkward silence sat between Lord Cranbourne and Miss Montagu as they waited for everyone to be settled comfortably in the waiting equipages. After it had stretched its length, they both spoke at the same moment.

"Miss—"

"Lord—"

They shared a rueful grin and it broke the tension that arced between them.

"Miss Montagu," Lord Cranbourne said. "Please forgive me for my boorish behaviour, earlier."

Marianne glanced quickly up at him, her brow furrowing. "I will, of course, sir. But I must admit, I am at a loss to understand it."

He flicked his whip and they moved off. "How could you when I hardly understand it myself?"

His honesty reassured her. A mischievous twinkle lurked in her eyes as she asked, "Are you prone to fits of the sullens?"

His lips quirked into a wry smile. "I had not thought so, but this house party is trying my patience somewhat."

Marianne thought she understood. It could not be easy having your lost love under your roof, after all. She would have liked to ask him directly about his feelings towards Lady Silchester, but knew that she could not. Instead she asked the question that had been bothering her all morning.

"I do not mean to be overly inquisitive, sir, but I do not comprehend why you were so cross that I discovered your philanthropic work. It is something to be admired, after all."

"I am happy that you think so, but I cannot in all good conscience take all the credit for the asylum. It was my mother's idea. She had long admired Lady Bamber's interest in improving conditions for the poor. I was happy to support her in her ambition to secure the future of orphaned young girls. She was a remarkable woman."

"I am sure she must have been," Marianne said softly. "But that does not explain your displeasure when I learned of your involvement in the scheme."

He glanced down at her, a smile lurking in his eyes. "You do like to cut to the chase, don't you, Miss Montagu?"

She grinned disarmingly. "But how else is one to find anything out?"

He suddenly laughed. "At the risk of disgusting you, ma'am, I shall match your candour. It did briefly cross my mind that you may have questioned my servants."

She considered this for a moment. "Well, I suppose I did. But only because Martha volunteered the information that she was one of your girls. And I thought…" She dropped her eyes. "Well, never mind what I thought."

His shoulders began to shake. "Miss Montagu! You thought she was one of my by-blows!"

Marianne glanced cautiously up at him and was relieved to see his eyes glinting with amusement.

"I *think* I know what that means. I wonder…" She glanced over her shoulder at his groom and coloured.

"Do not mind Hintley, Miss Montagu. He is the soul of discretion, and quite deaf to boot. But in answer to the outrageous question you were about to utter, no, not to my knowledge," he smiled. "But what business have you knowing of such things?"

"I don't really. It is just that after my mother died, I spent many years reading my way through my father's library. I may have picked up a few things that I did not perfectly understand at the time, but as I have grown older, some of them occasionally fall into place."

"You are fond of your father, I think."

She smiled a little mistily. "Oh, yes. He is the best of good men. I do miss him."

After a moment, Lord Cranbourne said, "It seems that you have lived your life through other people's observations of the world."

Marianne shrugged. "It could hardly have been otherwise. Until I was sent away to that dreadful seminary, I had hardly been anywhere."

"Was the seminary so very dreadful?"

Marianne sighed. "No, but it is the sort of place that likes to fit you into a certain mould, if you know what I mean? Everyone must talk in the same way, walk in the same way, and think in the same way."

"I know exactly what you mean, Miss Montagu. I have known many young ladies who fit your description."

They turned down a narrow lane, and soon came to a village. A cluster of cottages huddled around a green that was divided by a stream. All the houses looked as if they had stood there for centuries, but they were very well kept, and most had long neat gardens stretching in front of them, displaying an abundance of flowers and vegetables. Behind them an elegant church spire pierced the blue sky.

Marianne noticed that every passer-by politely curtsied or doffed their hats to Lord Cranbourne. He was clearly well respected here.

"This is the place I am named after," he said. "There are not many villages in this area, and this is one of the oldest."

They turned onto a track that took them up onto a wide open plain. At first it was cultivated, although not enclosed in any way, but before long they were surrounded by a wild rough grassland set beneath an expansive sky.

"I have never seen a place like this," Marianne said. "It feels so remote, so empty. I am sure if I walked up here, I would never find my way back again, there are no landmarks to guide you."

"You are not alone in your opinion, Miss Montagu. I have heard it called a dreary wasteland."

"I do not feel that," she said thoughtfully. "I am sure it has its own beauty and hides many secrets."

Lord Cranbourne's eyes warmed. "To me it speaks of freedom and has a timelessness that appeals to me. It has not been ruthlessly sculpted and shaped to fit any learnt ideal of beauty. It is, as you see, unchanged and unchanging. For thousands of years the feet of countless men and women have traversed this plain, and some have left their mark upon it."

He pointed his whip to where a long grassy mound suddenly rose from the land.

"I saw one or two of those on our journey here," Marianne said. "I thought how odd they looked, as if they did not belong in this setting."

"It is true that they are not a natural phenomena – if we were closer you would see the stones that mark the entrance – but they are very much part of the character of this landscape. They are the burial chambers of the ancient dead. When I was a child, I roamed these plains and could almost imagine their ghosts walked with me."

Marianne shuddered. "Were you not frightened?"

"No. I felt they watched over me. I think this was a place of great importance to them, and although I own much of this land, I feel as if it is still theirs, somehow. I would not change it, or disturb their peace. One of my ancestors investigated one of the barrows, but as soon as he divined its purpose, he shut it up again. I have had to disappoint more than one enthusiastic amateur archaeologist who has asked permission to excavate them."

"I think you were very right to do so," Marianne said quietly.

She suddenly gasped, her eyes widening as they reached the top of a gentle slope. In the distance a group of majestic standing stones were revealed. She felt the fine hairs on her arms rise and could almost believe the ghosts Lord Cranbourne had spoken of, were all around her.

The strange stones held a place of such eminence on the isolated plain, were so stately in their arrangement, and ancient in their origin, that she felt humbled in their presence.

"It must surely be a temple of some sort," she murmured.

He glanced down at her thoughtful brow, a small smile playing around his lips. "Perhaps, perhaps not. Whatever Lord Wedmore has gleaned from his no doubt extensive research about this place, it is all a mixture of fact, conjecture, and invention. The truth is lost in the mists of time and perhaps we should leave it there."

Marianne's brow furrowed. "But surely, sir, we all crave certainty?"

His lips twisted into a grimace. "Nothing in this life is certain, Miss Montagu."

They pulled up a little distance from the stones and Lord Cranbourne helped her down from the curricle. He nodded to his groom.

"Let the horses graze, Hintley."

Marianne stood transfixed by the great circle in front of her.

"They are like giant doorways," she whispered, as she regarded the lintels that capped the standing stones. "I am almost afraid to go under them in case I find myself in another world, another time."

"Come." Lord Cranbourne gently took her arm. "The others are not far behind, and the atmosphere of the henge will be lost once it is full of people."

Marianne allowed herself to be led into the inner circle. She slowly reached out a tentative hand to touch one of the stones, but then withdrew it.

"Do not be afraid." Lord Cranbourne took her hand and placed it against the cool surface. "It may or may not be a druidic temple, but I do not think you will find any ancient magic lurking in the stones. At least not any that would harm you."

Marianne felt him standing close behind her and stared at the large hand that covered her own. She closed her eyes and felt a strange tingling start in her hand and then move up her arm and into her body.

"There is magic here," she said softly. "I can feel it."

She felt his warm breath on her neck and shivered. "If there is, Miss Montagu," he murmured into her ear, "I think that you have wrought it."

She gasped as she thought his lips whispered against her neck, but then the touch was gone and she could not be certain she had not imagined it. His hand left hers and she felt him move away.

She remained there for a moment, her eyes closed, her hand still pressed against the stone. Her lips moved soundlessly as she sent a silent prayer to whatever gods or goddesses might look down on this otherworldly place.

Apart from Lord Ponsonby nearly suffering an apoplexy when he discovered his son's absence, the excursion was an undoubted success, in Marianne's eyes at least. She was pleased to observe the signs of a growing rapprochement between her aunt and Sir Robert, Lady Silchester seemed unusually subdued and attentive to her lord, and Lord Wedmore – once again given short shrift by Georgianna – continued to shower his attention on Miss Ponsonby.

Lord Cranbourne divided his attention equally amongst his guests. He seemed unusually relaxed and unbent so much that Miss Ponsonby managed a whole conversation with him without once giving the hideous laugh that overcame her whenever she was nervous.

He showed Marianne no extraordinary attention and so she soon persuaded herself that what she had thought might have been a brush of his lips against her neck, was no more than the whisper of the wind.

Mrs Stevens had provided a wide selection of cold meats, fruit, cakes, and wine, and so it was in a mellow mood that they all climbed back into their various carriages.

Marianne's early morning caught up with her and she allowed her thoughts to drift as Lord Cranbourne drove her back.

"You are very quiet, Miss Montagu," he finally said.

She looked up at her host and smiled sleepily. "I was thinking how much Mr Ponsonby would enjoy painting the stones. I am sure that he would capture their majesty and mystery."

Lord Cranbourne's brows winged upwards. "You have seen his work?"

"I have. I disturbed him painting in the temple this morning before breakfast. He has caught Cranbourne to perfection. I have advised him to show it to you when he has finished. I am sure you must admire it."

"Then I will look forward to judging it for myself," he said, a little stiffly.

Marianne turned eager eyes towards him. "You may have to encourage him to allow you to view it. He has no confidence in his ability at all. It is such a shame that Lord Ponsonby does not seem to appreciate his talent."

"You may be sure I shall do so, Miss Montagu. But tell me, were you alone for this

tête-à tête?"

"Yes," she said, surprised at the hint of censure in his tone. "It was very early. I had not expected to find anyone else in the gardens. But even Nancy did not seem to think there could be any harm in it."

"But then Nancy did not prevent you from following that cat either, did she?" he said, his soft tones in no way concealing his disapproval. "Whilst under my roof, Miss Montagu, I would prefer it if you would consider the proprieties at all times. You should not wander about alone when there are single gentlemen about."

Marianne felt her ire rise. They had seemed to develop a friendly understanding earlier, and she had felt happy that she need not guard her tongue in his company. But now he had reverted to the judgemental man she had thought him on their first acquaintance.

"Oh, do not speak to me, sir. You are unreasonable. If you wish to find fault with me, I am sure I will give you every opportunity to do so, but I hardly think that going for a stroll in your gardens deserves such reproach."

He took her at her word and an icy silence fell between them. Marianne was heartily glad when they turned, not many minutes later, into the park. She did not wait for him to help her down when he drew up in front of the house, but leapt from his curricle as soon as the horses came to a halt.

CHAPTER 16

L ord Cranbourne retreated to his study. He threw himself into his chair, leant his elbows on the desk, and dropped his head into his hands.

That was the second time today he had behaved to Miss Montagu in a priggish manner. What on earth was wrong with him? A few minutes thought shed some light on his conduct but brought him little solace. He was undoubtedly a fool. Miss Montagu was unaffected, open, and at times delightfully outrageous. She was also kind, naïve, and altogether adorable. The idea that she may have been gossiping with his servants should never have crossed his mind. But the fact remained, it had. He did not doubt her integrity but the irrational fear that he had been wrong in his estimation of her character had loomed before him, and it had been unpalatable. He really had not deserved that she forgive him so readily.

His reaction on discovering that she had been alone with young Ponsonby was easier for him to understand, but harder for him to accept. He had been jealous. The stolen moments they had shared amongst the stones had fuelled his desire for her. He should not have touched her. The moment he had laid his hand over hers, a frisson of desire had arced between them. Being the innocent that she was, she had named it magic. And it was, of a sort. He had been gripped by her spell and his lips had brushed against the vulnerable nape of her neck as if of their own accord. Only the sound of Lady Brancaster's voice had stopped him turning her around and crushing her lips beneath his own.

He was no longer a stripling and should be in full control of his emotions and desires, but they had easily slipped their leash in those few moments. How much more easily might Mr Ponsonby's feelings have over-taken him, especially if she had expressed her admira-tion for his talent with the same enthusiasm she had displayed when she had described it to him?

He would like to match her frankness and explain himself to her, but he could not without revealing his feelings towards her and he was as yet uncertain of her own. When he was not snapping her sweet little nose off, her manner towards him was friendly, confiding even, but whenever he tried to flirt with her in earnest, she withdrew.

He did not think she would forgive him quite so easily this time. Miss Montagu did not enjoy being criticised. He must make it up to her in some way. He raised his head from his hands, his eyes intent as the wisp of an idea wound through his mind. A slow smile spread across his lips and he reached for a sheet of paper and began to write.

A good half an hour later, he signed his missive. The sound of raised voices in the hallway disturbed him. Frowning, he pushed himself to his feet, strode over to the door, and flung it open.

The scene that met his eyes was an ugly one. Mr Ponsonby was cowering against the wall, a large canvas clutched to his chest. His father's face was puce with anger and Miss Ponsonby was clinging to his arm, ineffectually trying to pull him away.

"You will not disturb Lord Cranbourne, you conceited puppy! He will not be interested in your amateur dabbings. Give it to me. I will tear it to shreds!"

"No, Papa," Miss Ponsonby cried. "You must not."

Her father shook her off as he might an irritating insect and she fell to the floor, a shrill scream escaping her as she banged her cheek on a table that was set against the wall on her way down.

"Enough!" Lord Cranbourne's hard eyes and authoritative tone silenced Lord Ponsonby.

Lord Wedmore and Lord Silchester, who had been enjoying a game of cards in the library, came into the hall.

"Lord Wedmore, take Miss Ponsonby to see Mrs Stevens if you will. She will find something to put upon her cheek."

His eyes turned sternly upon Lord Ponsonby. "I would ask that you refrain from enacting such scenes in my house, sir. I would also prefer it if you did not destroy your son's painting before I have had the chance to see it."

"I would also very much like to see it," Lord Silchester said softly, coming forwards.

"Oh, have it your own way!" Lord Ponsonby snapped, throwing up his hands in disgust. "But do not feed his conceit with false flattery, sir, I implore you." He turned away on the words.

"A moment, Lord Ponsonby," Lord Cranbourne said, his tone more conciliatory. "Why do you not join us in my study, and we can look at it, all of us, together? Lord Silchester is, I believe, quite the connoisseur when it comes to art. "

"I would not care if you had a dozen connoisseurs in your house, sir. It is time he put off childish things and assumed the mantle of a man!" He stalked off in high dudgeon.

Lord Silchester gently took Mr Ponsonby's arm and ushered him into the room. "Come, let us see what has caused all this fuss and botheration."

With shaking hands, Mr Ponsonby slowly turned his canvas.

Both men studied it carefully for a few long minutes and then exchanged a glance. Unable to stand the suspense any longer, the tortured artist burst into speech. "It is no good, is it? Come, tell me, please, have I been deceiving myself?"

Lord Cranbourne stepped forwards, dropped a hand on his shoulder, and looked him steadily in the eye. "Calmly now, you gudgeon. It is excellent. I would know it anywhere. But it is more than that. I can almost smell the damp grass and hear the murmur of the river. I must have it."

"Do you really mean it, sir? You are not just being kind?"

Lord Cranbourne stepped away, a wry grin

twisting his lips. "I do not believe I am known for being kind."

"You have a most original touch with light," Lord Silchester said. "You have caught the early morning very well."

A beatific smile spread across Mr Ponsonby's pale face. "Thank you, both of you. Lord Cranbourne, please accept it as a gift."

"I will not," he said seriously. "You will be amply recompensed for your work. I think that if you continue with your painting, you will find you need the money."

"And you must not give it up," Lord Silchester said. "It would be such a waste if the world were to lose such a budding new talent."

"Thank you, sir," Mr Ponsonby said shyly. "I-I think you understand."

Lord Silchester smiled gently at him. "Oh, I do, young man, I do."

Nancy did not comment upon Marianne's mood of sad distraction, but was unusually gentle as she prepared her and Georgianna for dinner.

"There was quite a fracas downstairs this afternoon, miss," she said casually, as she carefully arranged a long strand of curls over Marianne's shoulder.

"Really?" she said, her tone lethargic.

"Poor Miss Ponsonby has got a horrible bruise on her cheek, and the beginnings of a black eye to boot."

Marianne's head snapped up. "Whatever happened?"

"Well, I can tell you. I have become quite friendly with one of the maids, and she heard everything. Must have had her ear pressed to the door mind you, for Mrs Stevens banished everyone from her room, even Lord Wedmore."

Marianne glanced at Georgianna. "Lord Wedmore?"

"Oh, he had nothing to do with it, miss. Lord Ponsonby was trying to stop Mr Ponsonby from showing Lord Cranbourne his painting. Threatened to tear it up. When Miss Ponsonby tried to stop him, he knocked her over."

Marianne gasped. "How very brutish of him. He did not tear it up, surely?"

"No, miss. Lord Cranbourne soon put a stop to that by all accounts."

"Thank goodness," she murmured.

A sharp rap sounded on the door.

"Come," Marianne called.

A maid hurried into the room. "I have a message for Lady Georgianna," she said, a trifle breathlessly, as if she had been running. "I tried her door first, but there was no one there."

"Obviously," murmured Nancy.

Marianne smiled at the maid. "No. She is here as you see, Martha."

The girl hurriedly handed it to her.

"Thank you, Martha," Georgianna said calmly.

Marianne's ennui abruptly deserted her. She watched her friend slowly read and re-read the message.

"Well?" she said impatiently.

Georgianna turned to her, a faint frown creasing her brow. "Lord Wedmore requests that I come to the blue saloon a little earlier than usual. He wishes to have some private conversation with me."

Marianne's eyes widened. "He surely cannot mean to offer for you after you have treated him with such disdain?"

Georgianna shook her head. "No, I do not think he would be so improper as to ask me without permission from my papa."

"I thought that he already had it," Marianne said, surprised.

Georgianna shook her head. "Not officially. There has been some talk between them that has led to an expectation of the request being made, but as yet, it has not been, as far as I know."

"How intriguing," Marianne said. "Will you go?"

"I must admit I am reluctant to do so," Georgianna said thoughtfully. "Yet perhaps it is not about me at all. It may not be a coincidence that his desire for a private audience comes so soon after this afternoon's dramatic events. And although I have had very little to do with Miss Ponsonby, I believe I would help her if it was within my power to do so."

"Your feelings do you credit," Marianne said gently.

Georgianna smiled wryly at her. "I know how difficult it is to be ridden over roughshod by ambitious parents. But I will not go down alone. If I am mistaken, and Lord Wedmore does mean to ask for my hand, your presence must surely prevent him from doing so."

Her eyes rose to meet Nancy's. "I am sure I do not need to ask you to turn a deaf ear to this conversation."

The maid bristled. "No, that you don't, my lady."

Georgianna smiled. "I thought not."

When the two young ladies quietly entered the blue saloon, they found Lord Wedmore pacing up and down murmuring to himself, as if trying to learn the lines from a poem or play.

Georgianna coughed and he came to an abrupt halt. As his eyes alighted on Marianne, he frowned.

"Miss Montagu, I do not wish to appear rude, but I have something of a very private nature to say to Lady Georgianna. Would you mind very much stepping out of the room for a moment?"

Marianne felt Georgianna's hand grip her wrist in a tight hold.

"I have no secrets from Miss Montagu," she said firmly.

Lord Wedmore glanced at the clock on the mantelpiece and seemed to come to a decision. "As you wish, Lady Georgianna. Please, sit down, ladies."

They both perched on the edge of a sofa and turned enquiring eyes upon him.

Lord Wedmore looked uncomfortable under their scrutiny. He eased a finger inside his neckcloth as if to loosen it and cleared his throat. After a few false starts, he took a deep breath and finally managed to begin the speech he had so carefully rehearsed.

"I suspect you are aware, Lady Georgianna, that there has been some discussion between your father and myself about the possibility of a union between us."

Marianne heard her friend's soft gasp and reached for her hand, wincing as Georgianna's fingers curled around hers in a vice-like grip.

"I was to have attended a house party at your home to become a little better acquainted with you, but as you know, circumstances rendered that an impossibility. It seemed that fate had intervened when you were invited to Cranbourne. But I would have needed to be insensate to not soon have realised that you did not desire a closer acquaintance."

A flush of pink crept into Georgianna's cheeks. Her evident embarrassment seemed to relieve his. His spoke with more authority and certainty as he continued.

"I do not wish for a reluctant bride, ma'am. I do not look for, or expect to find love in marriage, but I do require a mutual liking and respect at least. As you do not seem to feel either of these qualities, I felt it best that I inform you of the change in my intentions."

Georgianna's gaze dropped to the floor. "I thank you for your frankness, sir. I am aware that in my desire not to encourage you in any way, I may have been…" She paused and raised her eyes to his. "I *have* been cold towards you. I did not wish to disrespect you, sir, but neither did I wish to find myself wed before I had experienced anything of the world, or at least mingled in society a little. I hope you can under-stand and can find it in your heart to forgive my manners. I have judged you unfairly it would seem, and I sit before you humbled by my ignorance and your dignity in this most awkward of situations."

Lord Wedmore smiled quite gently at her. "You

had no need to use such tactics, you know. You only had to tell me of your feelings and I would have respected them."

"I thought that you were hand in glove with my parents, sir. I have made my feelings clear, but they did not heed them. How was I to know that you would?"

"I see," he said thoughtfully. "I shall write to your father, of course. I am sure he will be disappointed, but I assure you I shall not lay any blame at your door."

"You are very kind, sir," Georgianna said quietly.

"Not really," he said. "You see, I chose this moment to speak with you because this very afternoon I have offered for Miss Ponsonby and my proposal has been accepted. I did not wish the announcement to take you by surprise."

Georgianna smiled ruefully at him. "You have given me more consideration than I deserve, sir. Please accept my sincere congratulations."

"Thank you. You have done me a great service, Lady Georgianna. If you had not acted as you did, I may not have discovered how much I admire Miss Ponsonby." His brow darkened. "I had not meant to declare myself so soon, but when I saw what happened to her this afternoon, I threw caution to the wind. It is most unlike me to act in so precipitous a manner, but the sooner I can remove her from such a household, the better. That such a gentle—"

He broke off as the two most eminent members of that household entered the room. Marianne and Georgianna stood and moved a little away. Lady Ponsonby offered them the briefest of nods.

Any hopes she had of her daughter attaching Lord

Cranbourne had waned considerably over the last few days. It had not mattered how many times she had urged her to put herself forwards, he had shown very little interest, even though he had had every opportunity to do so. She could not understand it. She was sure her girl was just as beautiful as any other present and if not as high-ranking as Lady Georgianna, she was far more agreeable. Not that he had shown a particular interest in that direction, either. The only young lady he had distinguished in any way, was Miss Montagu, the daughter of a mere baronet. She was quite pretty, she supposed, although her nose was a little too short for her to be called beautiful. She could only conclude that he was amusing himself at his sister's expense, something he seemed to take great delight in.

She had watched her daughter's burgeoning friendship with Lord Wedmore with approval – one earl was as good as another, after all.

She came forwards, her face wreathed in smiles. "I am afraid that my daughter is a little shy of coming down this evening, Lord Wedmore. Her unfortunate accident has given her a most unsightly bruise. It is only temporary of course, her delicate skin is so fair, it has always bruised easily. We have decided it is better that we take her home tomorrow until it heals. We hope that you will visit us in a couple of weeks when she is herself again."

Lord Wedmore bowed a little stiffly. "I will, of course, visit you, ma'am. But if you wish me to wait merely because Miss Ponsonby's face is a trifle discoloured, I must inform you that it is quite unnecessary. It cannot weigh with me, your daughter has many other qualities that I admire."

"You are a man of sound sense, sir," Lord Ponsonby said. "Come with us tomorrow, by all means."

"Well, that is settled then." Lady Ponsonby smiled. "Now, come, sit with me, sir. I would like to know my future son-in-law a little better. I would be very interested to hear more of Wedmore House. Tell me, how does it compare with Cranbourne?"

Marianne smiled warmly at Georgianna. "Is it not wonderful? You need not worry any longer."

"Yes, it is, of course."

Marianne's brow wrinkled. "I thought you would be a little happier."

"Oh, I am happy, I assure you. But it would hardly be flattering to Lord Wedmore if I were to be cast into transports of delight by his announcement. Not that I am ever cast into transports of delight, it is not in my nature. Besides, my judgement has proven to be sadly lacking, Marianne. I made all sorts of assumptions about him based on my own fears, my estimation of myself, and my parents' view of the situation."

"Do not tell me, Georgianna, that now that he no longer wants you, your own feelings have changed?"

She laughed softly. "Hardly. We would not have suited. But I am beginning to realise that I have formed habits that I do not admire. Lord Wedmore is as fortunate as I am to have escaped this match. I am not yet fit to be anyone's wife. But enough about me, what has thrown you into the dumps?"

Most of the other guests had gathered since they

had been talking, and her eyes searched the room for Lord Cranbourne but did not find him.

"It is nothing," she murmured, as Mr Ponsonby approached them.

His eyes shone with happiness and he carried himself with a new confidence, his shoulders back and a spring in his step.

"You were right, Miss Montagu. Lord Cranbourne did like my painting. I don't know how to thank you."

"Then don't." She smiled. "It has been quite a day for you and your sister, it would seem."

"Lord, hasn't it just! Poor Lucinda. It is strange but she is always fierce in her defence of me, yet can never stand up for herself. I think she will be happy with Lord Wedmore. He is a little fusty perhaps, but she seems much more at ease with him than any other gentleman of her acquaintance."

"I hear you are to leave tomorrow, Mr Ponsonby. It is a shame, as I am convinced you would enjoy painting the circle of standing stones up on the plain."

Excitement flared in his eyes. "I have more to thank you for, than you know, Miss Montagu. Lord Cranbourne has invited me to stay on and has commissioned me to do just that. But that is not all. Lord Silchester has requested that I return with him to his home. Apparently he has several works of art he is sure I will wish to see and he would like me to paint Lady Silchester's portrait. I feel as if I must be dreaming."

"And your father has agreed to this?" she said, surprised.

"He is so pleased with Lucinda, that he has." He frowned and mimicked his father in an undertone. "At least one of my children knows their duty!" He grinned. "It may have helped that Lord Wedmore was present when I asked his permission. I heard my mother tearing a strip off him earlier. She said that if he had not yet given Lord Wedmore a disgust for us, she begged that he would not do so or he would ruin Lucinda's chances."

"I am very pleased for you," Marianne said.

Lord Cranbourne was putting the final touches to his cravat when his valet answered a knock at his door.

"If you please, ma'am, his lordship is not yet ready. I am sure—"

"Oh, get out of my way, Sallow," Lady Strickland said, brushing past him. She waited only for him to disappear into the dressing room before bursting into speech.

"Have you heard, Cranbourne, that Lord Wedmore has, this very afternoon, offered for Miss Ponsonby?"

He did not speak for a moment whilst he gently dropped his chin to acquire the desired creases in his neckcloth. Finally satisfied, he turned and regarded her with a satirical eye.

"I am sure I wish them both happy."

"I expect you do, it lets you off the hook nicely. When I think of how I condescended to befriend that scheming creature and now she will sit at my dinner table and preen herself on her success!"

"Oh, do stop ranting, Maria. I think you will find that it is my dinner table. Let this be a lesson to you not to interfere in my affairs. And do, please, ensure that you do not show that Friday face to our guests."

"I do not pretend to understand you, Cranbourne. I wash my hands of you, really I do."

"If only," he murmured provocatively.

Lady Strickland did not think this sally worthy of a response and rushed on. "If you really could not like Miss Ponsonby – and perhaps it is just as well that you did not – for I cannot approve of the Ponsonbys after that undignified fracas earlier, then you might have at least have shown an interest in Lady Georgianna. She must be one of the most beautiful girls I have ever seen, and of such a good family. She is a little proud, perhaps, but then so are you. She would know how to go on at Cranbourne, I am sure. But the only lady present you have condescended to be at all friendly to, is that little dab of a girl, Miss Montagu. That you are trifling with her, I have no doubt, but it is really too bad of you."

"But perhaps I am not trifling with her," he said softly.

"Do not be ridiculous, Cranbourne. I will not be taken in. What has she to recommend her, after all? Have you considered that if you do not settle down before you are much older, you will end up in Lord Silchester's predicament?"

He merely raised an eyebrow.

"Do not be obtuse, Cranbourne. He has a beautiful but much younger wife, who is heartily bored of him. If she does not create some sort of scandal before long, I will own myself amazed!"

"As she will not create it here, Maria, you need not concern yourself with the Silchesters. And although I am touched by your sisterly concern for my future happiness, as I have not reached thirty quite yet, I cannot help but feel it is a little premature. Console yourself with the thought that it is Lord Wedmore who is more likely to find himself in that position, although personally, I think they will do very well together. We have a lady underneath our roof at this very moment who was very happily married to an older man, after all."

His sister's bosom swelled, her sense of ill usage overcoming all restraint. "Oh, do not talk to me of Fanny Brancaster. She always was a flighty piece before she was married. And if you think I have forgotten the scandal that was hushed up before that timely and very fortunate event, you are much mistaken. I cannot imagine what possessed Lady Westbury to leave Lady Georgianna in her charge. There never was any love lost between them, after all. Perhaps I should write to her. I am fairly certain that if she was aware of the fact that Sir Robert Pinkington was sitting in Lady Brancaster's pocket, she would be most displeased."

Lord Cranbourne's eyes narrowed and he spoke with icy precision. "You have now gone your length, Maria. I am not at all sure of what you refer to, sister, and nor do I wish to know, but if I find that you have written such a spiteful letter or that any rumour of her aunt's past conduct comes to Miss Montagu's ears, you may be sure this will be the last time your feet cross the threshold of Cranbourne."

Her eyes widened and she blanched. Cranbourne might no longer be her home, but her connection with it still added to her consequence. "You would not!"

"Try me," he said softly.

Without saying another word, she turned and fled the room.

Lord Cranbourne sighed, and ran a hand through his hair. Damn, Maria. He had hoped to have a little conversation with Miss Montagu before dinner, but there would not now be time.

His glance rested on a ruby velvet curtain that hung on the wall. He stepped forwards and pulled the golden tassel that hung beside it. A family portrait was revealed. His eyes rested on his father, mother, and brother in turn, and then fell to the plaque that was embedded in the frame. It bore his father's favourite maxim – carpe diem.

"Perhaps you are right," he murmured.

CHAPTER 17

They had not long been seated at the dinner table, when Lord Cranbourne pushed back his chair and rose to his feet. All conversation stopped immediately.

"I would like to propose a toast to the happy couple who have this day made a commitment to each other. I am no scholar, but I believe it was Horace who warned us not to predict the future as it was for the Gods to decide our fate. I have had some reason to believe these words were wise. If it were not for an unfortunate twist of fate, I would not today stand before you as the Earl of Cranbourne. Believe me when I say that it was never my ambition and I could wish that it was not so. It seems cruel that my brother, who was a gentle, kind soul, should not stand here today. Instead, Horace advised that we should enjoy today, pour the wine, and not look too far ahead." He paused and smiled ruefully at the gentlemen present. "I must own that I may have taken these words a little too much to heart."

He waited for their subdued laughter to die down. "The last line, if I remember correctly, is *carpe diem quam minimum credula postero.* Pluck the day, put little trust in tomorrow. But I have come to realise that although I agree with the first sentiment, I find the second wanting. If we do not put any trust in tomorrow, our hopes and dreams are hollow. If we do not look to the future, what purpose has our today? So I would ask you all to raise your glass to Lord Wedmore, who has both plucked the day and put his faith in tomorrow."

He raised his glass, his eyes sweeping around the table, before dwelling for a moment on Marianne. "To the future!"

Marianne was moved by his speech. She took a small sip of wine and carefully replaced her glass, her vision momentarily blurred by unexpected tears. She bowed her head, raised her napkin, and dabbed at the corners of her lips whilst she blinked hurriedly to dispel them. His words about cruel fate had stuck a chord, and the look he had cast her had seemed to hold a strange mixture of apology and entreaty. She did not know what to make of it. Her heart urged her to hope that he now regretted his censure of her conduct, but her head warned her that he could be as capricious as the gods he spoke of.

It was perhaps fortunate that Mr Ponsonby, who was unusually animated, not to mention garrulous, gave her very little opportunity to dwell on such thoughts. But the strain of maintaining a polite steam of chatter took its toll, and by the time the ladies rose to leave the gentlemen to their port, she felt quite drained.

She caught up with Lady Brancaster in the hall. "I have a headache, Aunt. Would you mind very much if I retired?"

Lady Brancaster looked at her niece, concerned. "I thought you seemed a little subdued. Would you like me to come with you, my dear?"

"I do not wish to spoil your evening. I am sure a little rest is all that I require."

Miss Bragg's sympathetic gaze rested for a moment on her. "I am sure it is not at all surprising, this horrid heat is enough to give anyone a headache. It is probably why Lady Silchester did not come down to dinner."

"Would you like me to come up with you?" Georgianna asked.

Although Marianne valued her friend's insightful comments, she shook her head. It had occurred to her after their earlier conversation, that she also had some habits that she should overcome. One of them was not thinking before she reacted to a situation. She had been very quick to condemn Lord Cranbourne for suggesting that she should not wander about his estate unescorted. But the excited light that had brightened Mr Ponsonby's eyes when he had approached her before dinner, had reminded her of the unsteadiness of temper he had displayed at the temple, and she had realised that his concern may not have been completely unwarranted. She felt very much in need of a period of quiet reflection to consider all that had passed between them.

"Thank you, but I do not feel up to company at the moment," she murmured.

"Very well, off you go," Lady Brancaster said.

"But do not rise with the dawn tomorrow. Stay abed and drink some chocolate. It always works wonders for me. I shall come to your room for a nice, quiet cose before breakfast."

As Marianne reached the corridor that led to her room, she saw Martha scurrying towards her. She smiled at the girl. Martha stopped and dipped into a respectful curtsy.

"I've just put a warming pan in your bed, miss," she said. "But seeing you puts me in mind of something. When I took Miss Ponsonby's in, earlier, she said that if I should see you, I should tell you that she would be most gratified if you paid her a visit."

Marianne's brows rose in surprise. "Thank you, Martha. I shall, of course, do so, but I do not know precisely where she is. Could you perhaps show me the way?"

"O'course, ma'am. Follow me."

She led her down a flight of stairs and along the hallway in which she had first encountered her. One of the many doors that faced onto the corridor opened, and a slight figure came onto the landing. His furrowed brows and pursed lips gave his narrow face a look of deep disapproval. He offered Marianne a slight bow as they hurried past.

"That is Sallow, miss," she whispered. "Lord Cranbourne's valet. Very high in the instep, he is."

They turned a corner and came to a halt.

"This is Miss Ponsonby's room, miss."

Marianne smiled. "Thank you. That will be all, Martha."

She knocked on the door gently, in case Miss Ponsonby should be asleep. When no response was forthcoming, she turned and began to move away. She heard a slight click and looked over her shoulder. She gasped. Miss Ponsonby was hardly recognisable. Her blonde locks were hidden under a cap, her cheek was hideously discoloured, and her eye so swollen she could hardly open it.

Even as her lips opened to voice her dismay, Miss Ponsonby put her finger to her own, and opened the door a little further.

Marianne slid into the room and closed the door softly behind her.

"You poor thing," she murmured.

"We must be quiet," Miss Ponsonby whispered. "My maid is in the dressing room and she has orders not to allow anyone to see me. I think Mama is afraid that if Lord Wedmore catches sight of me now, he will have second thoughts about his offer."

Marianne smiled kindly at her. "She has learned of her mistake. It is to his credit that he is not at all concerned about it. He informed Lady Ponsonby that you have many other qualities that he admires."

Miss Ponsonby blushed. "I am sure I have no idea what they may be. But I wished to thank you, Miss Montagu, for your advice to be myself. I even found Lord Cranbourne easier to deal with when I was not always trying to remember what I should or should not say."

"I am pleased that you found that to be the case," Marianne said wryly.

"I have never thought about anything very deeply before, you see," Miss Ponsonby said. "I am not at all used to forming opinions on anything but the latest fashions. But I am learning, and Lord Wedmore encourages me."

Marianne took her hands. "I hope you will be very happy."

"I am sure I will be. To think I will soon be mistress of my own home. It is an exciting yet daunting thought, but Lord Wedmore assures me that Wedmore Hall is not built on quite the same scale as Cranbourne, and I must say that I am glad. It would be very unnerving to run this household, I think."

"Oh, it is only bricks and mortar, after all," Marianne said. "It is the people that make a place, and I think you will find that if you have a good house-keeper who you are happy to let guide you, you will do very well, Miss Ponsonby."

A rustling sound came from the dressing room.

"You had better go, Miss Montagu. We are leaving early in the morning, so I shall say goodbye now. Would you mind giving me your direction so I can write to you?"

"Not at all." Marianne reached into her reticule and retrieved a folded piece of paper and a pencil. She hastily scribbled her address, tore the paper, and handed it over. "I would very much like to hear how you go on."

The sound of footsteps in the dressing room sent her hurrying to the door. She glanced over her shoulder as she opened it. "Goodbye, Miss Ponsonby, and good luck."

As Lady Strickland had made it abundantly clear that

she did not expect the gentlemen to linger over their port, after a few toasts of a slightly more indelicate nature, they trailed out of the dining room.

Lord Silchester hung back a little. "My good lady and I will also be leaving tomorrow, Cranbourne," he said. "Lady Silchester is not feeling quite the thing."

"I am sorry to hear that," Lord Cranbourne said politely.

His guest gave a gentle laugh. "Come, my friend, admit it, you are mightily relieved."

Lord Cranbourne coloured, but even as a denial rose to his lips, Lord Silchester continued.

"Oh, I am aware that you are far too well mannered to say so, but please do not deny what we both know to be the truth. I would ask you not to judge Melissa too harshly, however. Her lot is not an easy one, I assure you. If she does not feel wanted, desired, and admired, life holds little meaning for her."

"Why did you come, sir?" Lord Cranbourne said, after a moment.

"My lady is more brittle than you suppose, Cranbourne. She has not been quite right ever since she gave birth to my second son. She is often subject to fits of melancholy and dejection. They seem to last for a little longer each time. I think she has sustained herself by creating the myth that you also suffer, from an unending love for her."

Lord Cranbourne frowned. "I assure you, sir, that I have given her no reason—"

Lord Silchester touched his arm lightly. "Hush, my boy. I know it. She needed no more reason than your continued single state to weave a tale of heartbreak and unrequited love in her confused mind. I came because I felt her obsession had become increasingly unhealthy and hoped that by visiting Cranbourne she would somehow be jolted back to reality. Lady Strickland had intimated that she would not be at all surprised if you put in an appearance before the house party came to an end, and I felt fairly certain that she would discover her belief had foundations of sand and she would need my support. And so it has proven. She is very unhappy, my boy, and is to be pitied."

"So are you, I think, sir," he said gravely.

Lord Silchester smiled. "Do not waste your pity on me, Cranbourne. I do not look to Melissa for my happiness. I have my art, my boys, and my friends to sustain me. I married knowing that there would be no love in our marriage. It was perhaps, a selfish act, and I must and do bear the consequences."

Lord Cranbourne frowned as Sallow rushed into the room. His eyes widened as he saw Lord Silchester. He gulped. "My lord, I must have a private word with you."

"It must wait until later," Lord Cranbourne said. "I do not know what you think you are about to disturb me in this way."

The valet's eyes darted between his master and his guest.

Lord Silchester smiled gently at the man. "I can see that my presence has made you uncomfortable, but if this concerns Lady Silchester, you may speak freely in front of me, I assure you."

∼

As Marianne made her way back to her room, she heard a strange noise, half laugh and half sob. Her step faltered and she sniffed as an acrid smell assailed her nostrils. Glancing down, she saw wisps of smoke curling under the door she had seen Sallow come through, earlier.

She hastily threw it open and rushed into the room. A curtain that hung beside a painting, smouldered and burned, and a candle lay extinguished on the floor beneath it. Her eyes scanned the room and she hurried over to a basin of water that sat on a dressing table. Snatching it up she rushed back to the curtain and threw the contents of the basin over the burgeoning flames. As they flickered and died, she opened a window, tugged at an undamaged part of the curtain until it all came away from the wall, and threw it out into the garden.

"Let it burn," came a sleepy slurred voice from the bed. "Let it all burn."

Marianne spun around and for the first time saw the figure lying on the bed. Lady Silchester wore a white nightgown, her hair was unbound, and her feet bare. As she drew closer to the bed, she saw that the two eyes that regarded her were unfocused.

"Who is it?" She frowned. "Come closer, I cannot see you properly."

Marianne perched on the edge of the bed. "Lady Silchester, you are not yourself," she said gently. "Let me get you some help."

She jumped as Lady Silchester's long white fingers suddenly grasped her arm, and with a surprising show of strength, she pulled her down until their faces were only inches apart.

"He will not marry you," she hissed. "You are nothing, a nobody, a little country miss. It is me he has always loved, me and only me, do you understand?"

Marianne flinched as specks of spittle sprayed her face, yet the strange mixture of bewilderment, pain, and anger that sounded in Lady Silchester's voice and momentarily brightened her eyes, stirred sympathy in her breast.

"Yes," she said softly, "everyone knows it is you that he loves."

Lady Silchester suddenly flung her away. "You lie!" she cried. "I am nothing to him."

She rolled onto her side and closed her eyes, as if the exertion had exhausted her. "I am nothing," she whispered. "Nothing."

Even as a tear leaked from beneath her closed lids, her breathing deepened and Marianne realised that she was asleep.

She reached out a slightly unsteady hand and gently stroked her long, golden hair. "You poor, unfortunate lady," she murmured.

~

"Out with it, man," Lord Cranbourne snapped.

Sallow rushed into speech. "It is Lady Silchester, my lord. She wandered into your chamber in her nightgown as I was putting some of your things away. When I told her she had the wrong room, she just smiled strangely at me and began to wander about. She stopped in front of the family portrait and started murmuring, 'Why can't I see? Is it him?' I thought I had better come and fetch you, sir. When I heard you talking to someone, I waited outside but the more I thought on it, the more I realised that she seemed queer in her attic." He glanced at Lord Silchester. "No offence meant, my lord."

"And none taken," he said. "She has been taking laudanum to help her sleep, but she sometimes becomes a trifle confused."

Sallow looked relieved. "That would explain it, sir."

"Thank you, you did very well, Sallow," Lord Cranbourne said. "You can leave it with me and Lord Silchester, and not a word to a soul."

Sallow looked deeply offended at the suggestion he might lower himself enough to gossip with anyone, but bowed and left the room.

"I told her maid to keep a close eye on her," Lord Silchester said quietly as they mounted the stairs. "But she can become quite devious if her mind is set upon something."

When they entered his chamber the smoke had cleared but the smell of burning still hung in the air. Both gentlemen's eyes were drawn to the scorch marks on the wall.

"I am sure it was an accident. At least I was able to save the painting."

Lord Cranbourne's head snapped around and his brows rose in surprise as he saw Marianne standing calmly by his bed.

"Miss Montagu!"

She dipped her head. "Lord Cranbourne, Lord Silchester. I am sure you are both wondering what I am doing here."

"Saving the day, by the looks of it," Lord Silchester said, with a sad smile.

"I would not go that far," she said quietly. "But it was fortunate that I passed this way on the way back from Miss Ponsonby's room. I smelt and saw the smoke before the flames had really taken hold." She inclined her head towards the open window. "The curtain is in the garden."

"Never mind the curtain," Lord Cranbourne said, crossing the room to her side. "Have you hurt your hands?"

He took them in his own, only satisfied with her assertion that she had not, when he had given them a close examination.

As his eyes rose to meet hers, they paused as he saw the series of small red marks on her arm just below her short puffed sleeve.

Lord Silchester's keen eyes were also upon them.

"I am sorry if you are hurt, my child. My wife does not always know her own strength when she has one of her turns."

Marianne shook her head. "It is nothing, sir. I mark easily, and she was not herself. She became quite agitated, but is sleeping now."

Lord Cranbourne looked down at the woman who had once occupied his dreams. How he had yearned to see her with her hair unbound, asleep in his bed. Now, as he noted the purple shadows beneath her eyes, made even starker by her preternaturally pale face, he felt nothing but pity.

He suddenly stepped forwards, bent, and lifted her into his arms.

"Miss Montagu, could you go ahead please and make sure there is no one about?"

"Of course."

He waited for her to reach the corner and nod, before striding quickly down the landing. He nodded at a door. Marianne opened it and went ahead of him to turn down the bed.

"Thank you, both of you. I am sure I can rely on your discretion," Lord Silchester said quietly. He suddenly appeared even more stooped than usual and his complexion had a grey tinge. "I still hope that she will recover, in time."

Lord Cranbourne frowned. "I am sorry if I am responsible for her deterioration. I would have treated her more gently if I had known."

"But then you would have fuelled her delusions, my boy. A few days' rest at home will see her much improved. The boys adore her and usually raise her spirits. I am aware that you have asked young Ponsonby to paint the henge, but if you don't mind, I'll take him with me, she will enjoy having her portrait painted."

"Of course, the stones are not going anywhere, after all."

They all turned as a series of sharp raps sounded on the dressing room door. Lord Silchester crossed the room, turned the key that was in the lock, and opened the door.

A harassed looking maid stood on the threshold. "I am sorry, my lord. She was very quiet tonight, but when I went to put her things away, she locked me in. I had no idea there was a key. I certainly hadn't seen one."

"Do not worry, Phipps, I do not blame you. But check the room for laudanum, would you? I am fairly certain she has been taking more than is good for her."

The maid nodded and began rifling through the drawers of the dressing table.

Lord Cranbourne's eyes met Marianne's. She nodded and moved towards the door.

"Wait for me, Miss Montagu. I will escort you to your room."

As she closed the door softly behind her, he dropped a hand on the older man's shoulder. "If there is ever anything that I can do…"

Lord Silchester briefly covered his hand with his own. Lord Cranbourne was relieved to see the twinkle again lurking in his eyes.

"What you can do, Cranbourne, is grasp the happiness that lies before you with both hands. Do not let that remarkable young lady slip through your fingers."

He found Miss Montagu waiting for him a little way down the corridor. There was much he would like to say to her, but it was too soon and he would not ruffle the admirable composure that had marked all her actions this evening. She was the first to break the delicate silence that hung between them.

"I was not snooping, sir, I assure you."

He looked down at her ruefully. "That the thought I would think any such thing even crossed your mind, rebukes me for my past behaviour far more than any harsh words could. I am very grateful for your intervention, Miss Montagu. You have saved much that is dear to me."

She blushed adorably and he was relieved to find they had reached her door or his good intentions may well have been overridden by the sudden desire to sweep her into his arms. Instead, he took one of her little hands in his, and raised it to his lips.

"Good night, and thank you."

CHAPTER 18

Marianne floated into her room, a tremulous smile on her lips. Admiration had shone clearly in the eyes that had held hers as he had kissed her hand. She pulled off her glove and placed her own lips against the spot that his had heated. She sat at her toilet table and stared at her reflection in the glass, slowly pulling out the pins that held her hair. As she reached for her brush, she knocked her reticule onto the floor. She had not fastened it properly after hastily scribbling her direction for Miss Ponsonby and the paper she had hurriedly stuffed back in, fell to the floor.

She picked it up, and saw the four words that Miss Bragg had scribbled when they had played Bouts-Rime. *Thought, must, naught, trust.* She stared at the words until they began to dance before her eyes, and then murmured, "*A moment's thought, reflect I must, it could mean naught, yet should I trust?*"

As Nancy just then bustled into the room she had

no further time to reflect until she tumbled into bed. Yet she found her memory curiously reluctant to reach beyond that moment outside her door, and soon fell into a deep sleep, a small smile playing about her lips.

She awoke unusually late the following morning, and had only just plumped up her pillows and sunk back against them when her aunt came into the room.

"Oh, good," Lady Brancaster said. "You have followed my advice. I am convinced that getting up at the crack of dawn as you do, must be injurious to your health."

"That is a very elegant dressing gown, Aunt Fanny," Marianne said, smiling sleepily.

Lady Brancaster glanced down at her dark blue silk robe, which was scattered with exotic looking blooms. "I suppose it is," she said. "Lord Brancaster liked to see me in pretty things."

She set the cup of chocolate she was carrying down on the bedside table, and climbed in next to her niece.

"Isn't this nice?" she sighed. "I don't know how it comes about, but we really have had very little opportunity to spend any time alone together."

"But then so much has happened in such a short span of time," Marianne said quietly.

"Has it?" Lady Brancaster said, looking at her closely. "Do you mean in general or since we have arrived here?"

"Since I arrived in Cheltenham," Marianne said.

Lady Brancaster looked a little disappointed. "Well, yes, I suppose it has." She sipped her chocolate thoughtfully for a moment. "Is that why you felt a little peaky, yesterday, do you think? Or is there perhaps something you would like to share with me?"

When Marianne said nothing, Lady Brancaster reached for her hand. Her eyes rested for a moment on the faint red smudges that still marked her wrists. "I may have been a little hard on you before, my love, but rest assured, I will not fly into the boughs at anything you may wish to confide in me. I am very fond of you and my only wish is to see you happy. You are such a dear, sweet, child."

Marianne returned her clasp but said in a small voice, "I have not been a dear, sweet, child to my step-mother." She shook her head as she saw her aunt about to launch into a no doubt scathing attack on the woman. "No, Aunt Fanny, please listen. I have come to realise that I never gave her a chance. I had been spoilt by Papa's attention and liberal ways. He rarely found any fault with me, and so I did not think there was any fault to be found. But I was anything but kind to her, and I provoked her at every opportunity. My reactions to her were coloured by a resentment I never feel when you reprimand me."

Lady Brancaster looked at her intently. "I see."

Marianne smiled gently. "I hope that you do. For I have also influenced your feelings towards her. Neither of us wished to see Mama replaced by anyone. But that was hardly fair on Papa or Simon, was it? What would have become of them when I..." she paused, "*if* I marry?"

Marianne's eyes were downcast and so she did not see the tears that suddenly brightened her aunt's.

"Oh, Marianne. You put me to shame. You are very right, my dear sister would not have wished Frederick to be lonely – I am only too aware of how miserable that makes one – or Simon to grow up without a mother." A puzzled expression soon replaced her penitent one, however. "But did he have to choose such a dowdy—"

"No, Aunt. I will hear no more in that vein."

Lady Brancaster's brows shot up.

Marianne raised her eyes and smiled gently at her. "I think he purposefully chose someone who would not remind him of Mama or fall in love with him."

She was interested to see a delicate flush steal over her aunt's cheeks. "I think it very kind in him. It must be uncomfortable to love someone who does not return the feeling."

"Yes," Lady Brancaster murmured. "I suppose it is."

After a moment, Marianne asked the question that was uppermost in her mind. "Aunt, how *do* you know when you are in love?"

A gentle smile curved her aunt's lips and a misty look dimmed her eyes. "Oh, in a dozen small ways. The way your heart beats a little faster when you see him, the odd feeling that something is missing when he is not there." She suddenly laughed. "The way he can infuriate you like no other or make you behave in a manner quite unlike yourself."

"I see," Marianne said, her brow wrinkling. "But how do you know if he loves you?"

"That is not quite so easy to determine. Men are such complicated creatures. They often seem to do or say something that in no way reflects their true feelings. I believe it is because they have not been taught to admire the gentler feelings. Anger can mask jealousy, coldness can hide hurt."

She suddenly turned and took both of Marianne's hands. "I will not enquire too closely as to why you are asking me these questions, my love, for I know how difficult it can be for others to make your mind up for you. But I will just say this, if you think you have an opportunity to be happy, take it."

Marianne withdrew her hands and threw her arms around her aunt. "Thank you," she whispered. "And please, Aunt Fanny, if you also have such an opportunity, I urge you to take it."

By the time they came down to sample the remnants of the breakfast buffet, the Silchesters, Ponsonbys, and Lord Wedmore had already taken their leave. Only Lady Georgianna and Lady Strickland were still at the table, as Miss Bragg had breakfasted much earlier.

"I hope you are feeling better, Miss Montagu," Lady Strickland said, her eyes as cold as her tone.

"Yes, thank you, ma'am," Marianne said politely.

Lady Strickland gave a rather sour smile. "We must not expect the gentlemen to join us today," she informed them. "They have gone to fish the river."

The butler entered the room and laid a letter beside Georgianna.

"Thank you, Wilmot." She broke the seal and began to read, her expression blank. When she had finished, she folded it neatly, placed it by her plate, and took a sip of her coffee.

The suspense proved too much for Lady Strickland. "Well, Lady Georgianna? Have you news?"

Her cool eyes rested for a moment on her hostess.

"I do, ma'am," she said in a colourless tone. "It seems my brother has fully recovered and my mama wishes me to return home. She is sending a carriage and my maid. They will arrive tomorrow and I am expected to leave, immediately. She wishes me to thank both you and Lady Brancaster for your kind hospitality."

"Oh, I see. And so it seems our little house party is nearing its end." Lady Strickland glanced pointedly in Lady Brancaster's direction. Unfortunately, that lady seemed to be suddenly afflicted with deafness and gave no indication that she had heard the remark.

Lady Strickland turned back to Georgianna. "I quite understand that your poor mama is probably so worn down that she has had no time to write and thank me herself, but I shall write to her this afternoon, and would be most grateful if you would take my letter to her."

"Of course, ma'am."

Lady Strickland inclined her head graciously. "You may be sure I will inform her of how very impressed I am by you, Lady Georgianna. Your manners are all that they should be."

"Thank you, Lady Strickland. You are too kind."

"I am very much afraid that that is only one of several things that I must attend to today, so I must leave you to entertain yourselves, ladies."

This announcement was received with relief in every quarter. As the day was again fine, Lady Brancaster asked Wilmot if he could arrange for a blanket and some chairs to be set out under one of the trees in the park. Lady Brancaster and Miss Bragg settled themselves in the shade, whilst Georgianna and Marianne took a stroll.

"Do you think Lord Westbury has already received Lord Wedmore's letter?" Marianne asked her friend.

Georgianna shrugged. "If it has not reached Avondale already, it most certainly will have by the time I arrive there."

"How do you think he and your mother will receive the news?"

"I think it is Mama who will be most displeased. But what can she do after all? If Lord Wedmore keeps his promise not to lay any blame at my door, and Lady Strickland sings my praises, she can have very little to say."

"I will miss you," Marianne said gently.

Georgianna's lips widened into a genuine smile. "And I you. But I hope you will write to me with some exciting news, before long."

Marianne slowed and kicked at a clump of grass in front of her. "I do not know. I am not at all sure you are right."

"But you are certain of your own feelings? I assume he was the cause of your headache last night?"

"Yes," Marianne admitted. "I do not always understand him."

Georgianna frowned. "You do not still think he is in love with Lady Silchester, surely? All the evidence is against it."

"No, I do not think that," Marianne said. She considered her aunt's description of being in love. "And I am sure of my own feelings, I think."

Georgianna laughed. "I do not think I would enjoy being in love, the feelings it seems to imbue in its victims, appear to be confusing and contradictory."

As they returned to Lady Brancaster and Miss

Bragg, they saw a carriage pull up in front of the house.

Incurably nosy, Lady Brancaster got to her feet the better to see the new arrival. As the carriage moved off a lady could be seen mounting the shallow steps, accompanied by a footman.

"Oh, if I am not much mistaken, that is Lady Bamber," she said. "We must go and pay her our respects."

When they entered the sunny morning room that was used for informal visits, a small lady, with smiling hazel eyes got to her feet.

"Lady Brancaster, Miss Bragg, what an unexpected treat to find you here."

Once the introductions had been made and they had all sat down, Lady Brancaster said, "We were surprised to find ourselves here, but we met Lord Cranbourne in Cheltenham, and he kindly invited us to join Lady Strickland's house party."

"Cheltenham?" Lady Bamber said, her eyes sharpening. "And did you perhaps see my son there?"

"Indeed we did," said Lady Brancaster. "We saw him at the pump room, of course, but also at a ball, and he joined us on a day out in the countryside. He very generously provided the delicacies for an al fresco nuncheon we enjoyed."

Lady Bamber blinked. "Horace went to a ball without me dragging him there? And accompanied a party of ladies to an al fresco nuncheon?"

Her eyes turned to the younger ladies of the party. "Did he dance with you?" she enquired, a trifle warily.

"His foot would not allow it," Marianne said.

"Of course it would not." Lady Bamber

murmured, and then smiled fondly. "It was probably just as well, otherwise I think you would have found your toes shockingly bruised."

"Although I did not dance with Sir Horace, I sat one out and bore him company."

"How very kind of you," she said gently. "And did he talk with you?"

Marianne had liked Lady Bamber on sight, and laughed. "Of course he did. It would have appeared very strange if he had not, after all."

"Then I suppose you have formed a very odd impression of him."

"Not at all. I found it very enjoyable to speak with him."

"Really? Well that is a first."

"I also enjoyed his company," Lady Georgianna said, a glint of amusement in her eyes. "We found we had an interest in fossils in common."

Lady Bamber's eyes grew round. "Well, perhaps I shall forgive him for running off to Cheltenham, after all. It seems it did him a great deal of good."

"His foot was also much improved, I think," Miss Bragg said, gently.

"I am very pleased to hear it." Lady Bamber smiled. "Especially as he has seen fit to pay his brother a visit. Loftus does not approve of idleness. He will find a hundred things for him to do and it serves him right. It was an extraordinary coincidence how quickly his foot began to ail him after he heard his cousin was going to pay us a visit."

"He does not like his cousin?" Marianne asked.

"He does not like anyone he thinks I might like him to marry," Lady Bamber said dryly. "I do so hate to be an interfering, matchmaking mama, but if he will not make any effort himself to find a bride, what am I to do?"

"Indeed, it must be very difficult," Lady Brancaster sympathised.

Lady Bamber sighed. "Yes, indeed it is. But in this case, it was probably for the best. Jane would not have done for him at all. Indeed, I found her very tiresome and was not at all sorry when it was time for her to return home."

Lady Strickland came into the room. "I am sorry to have kept you waiting, Lady Bamber." She came to a halt and raised her brows. "Oh, I see our visitors were here before me."

"Please do not apologise, Lady Strickland. It has been very pleasant to renew old acquaintances."

"Yes, well, I am happy that you have been adequately entertained."

"Indeed, I have."

The conversation turned to general chitchat, and it was not long before Lady Bamber took her leave.

The ladies returned to the garden. Marianne and Georgianna lay back on the blanket and amused themselves finding creatures in the puffs of white cloud that chased each other across the sky.

"That one is definitely a horse," Marianne murmured.

"No, it is clearly a dragon," Georgianna said. "Miss Bragg, you must decide."

"Very well." She pushed her needle into the handkerchief she was embroidering, laid it on her lap and squinted up at the sky. "It is neither," she said confidently. "It is a dog."

Both girls dissolved into giggles.

"Aurora, when are you going to get some spectacles?" Lady Brancaster said, smiling. "It could be either a horse or a dragon, although I think it is a little more like a horse, but it looks nothing like a dog!"

Miss Bragg bent over her sewing again. "I know I need spectacles, dear, but they are so very aging."

Marianne sat up and looked up at Miss Bragg in some surprise. "Miss Bragg! I would never have guessed that you cared about such things!"

Miss Bragg sighed. "I know, it is ridiculous. But long ago, when I was just a girl, a gentleman once told me that I had the most remarkable eyes. I am sure it was the nicest compliment I ever received, and I am loathe to cover them up."

"He was right," Marianne said. "I have never seen eyes of such a light grey before."

"Who was he?" Georgianna asked.

Miss Bragg's remarkable eyes lost their usual clarity as she gazed into the past. "It was Mr Crumpton. He came as a young man to be the vicar of our small parish."

"I do believe you were in love with him," Marianne murmured.

"I was," Miss Bragg said softly. "And he with me."

"Why did you not marry?"

Miss Bragg returned to the present and she said in a matter of fact way. "Smallpox. He visited a sick family who had recently come from London and caught it from them."

Lady Brancaster briefly covered her hand with her own. "You were very unfortunate, Aurora."

"Perhaps, but it was all a long time ago. And I

have been very fortunate in my friends and family, so I shall not complain."

"You never do," Lady Brancaster said.

"No, but I must admit I do enjoy a wedding if the couple are suited. It warms my heart."

CHAPTER 19

With the loss of so many guests, two leaves were removed from the dining table and dinner had a more informal feel. Although it earned him a frown from his lady, Lord Strickland did not hesitate to address the gentleman who sat across the table from him.

"I say, Sir Robert, you missed a fine day's fishing."

"Oh, you did not go?" Lady Brancaster said, surprised.

Sir Robert looked a little sheepish. "No, I visited the cathedral in Salisbury."

"But why all the secrecy?" she asked. "I believe I would like to see it myself."

"As would I," added Miss Bragg. "Is it worth a visit, do you think?"

Sir Robert gave her a grateful smile. "Indeed it is. I shall take you both tomorrow. But remember what I said in Cheltenham, Lady Brancaster, about it being much better to rely on a visitor who has formed a pleasing impression of a place before you visit it yourself. Thought I'd better give it a look over before I dragged you there."

Her eyes softened. "That was very thoughtful of you, Sir Robert." She turned to Marianne. "Do you think you would enjoy it, my dear?"

"I might, but I would rather wait with Lady Georgianna until her carriage arrives, if you do not object?"

"Of course I don't." Lady Brancaster frowned. "Perhaps we should postpone our visit."

"I am sure that is not necessary," Miss Bragg said gently. She glanced respectfully at the lady who sat at the end of the table. "I am sure we can leave Miss Montagu and Lady Georgianna in Lady Strickland's capable hands."

"Indeed you can," she said, a trifle stiffly. "I shall ensure that Lady Georgianna receives all the attention that her position deserves."

"Well, that is settled then." Sir Robert looked pleased.

"Thank you, Lady Strickland." Lady Brancaster said. "I am sure I need have no worries about either of the girls now that I know you will watch over them both."

After an evening of quiet conversation, the party broke up quite early. But before Marianne retired, Lord Cranbourne managed to find the opportunity to snatch a few quiet words with her.

"I must thank you for your discretion, Miss Montagu. It seems last night's affairs have been hushed up quite effectively. My poor, loyal valet has taken the blame for leaving a candle burning beneath the curtain, although it is a hard blow for his not inconsiderable pride to take."

She smiled shyly up at him. "I would not have that poor lady's affliction become the topic of gossip or speculation, sir."

"I know it," he said, smiling at her in a disconcertingly warm manner. "Perhaps you would walk with me in the gardens tomorrow, once Lady Georgianna has left?"

"Yes, I will look forward to it," she murmured.

Lady Strickland's strident tones interrupted them. "What are you about, Cranbourne? Let that poor girl get to bed. Can you not see that Lady Brancaster is waiting for her?"

That night, Marianne's dreams were full of Lord Cranbourne. She dreamed they were wed by a druid with a long white beard and loose flowing robes in a pagan ceremony amidst the stones, with the gods she had prayed to smiling down benevolently upon them. It was most reluctantly that she awoke when Nancy bustled in and drew her curtains.

"Are you ailing for something, miss?" she asked. "It's not like you to sleep in so long."

Marianne rubbed the sleep from her eyes and sat up. "I do not think I have ever felt better, Nancy."

"Well, I'm glad to hear it, miss. Now come along, you don't want to be late for breakfast on Lady Georgianna's last day. She's all packed and ready. It'll be a shame to see her go. It took me a while to get used to her reserved ways, but she's a nice young lady for all that."

Marianne climbed out of bed and smiled at her

maid. "She is. Beneath that cool exterior, she has a good heart, Nancy."

By the time they came downstairs, Sir Robert's party were on the point of departure.

Her aunt pinched her cheek. "You are turning into a slug-a-bed, after all."

Georgianna's carriage arrived shortly after breakfast. Marianne just caught a glimpse of her stern-looking maid before she was ushered away by Mrs Stevens for some refreshment before she continued her journey.

"You can be sure she will manage to extract whatever information she can in the time it takes her to swallow a cup of tea," Georgianna said dryly.

"You need not worry," Marianne assured her. "Mrs Stevens is nobody's fool and will say all that is correct, but she will not countenance gossip about the guests, of that I am certain."

Georgianna looked down at her, affection and admiration warming her eyes. "How is it you have been here only a few days and already know the housekeeper, not to mention some of the servants' names?"

Marianne grinned at her friend. "It is because I have deplorably open manners and have no idea of my station, I am sure."

Marianne was moved when Georgianna embraced her briefly before she climbed into her carriage, her eyes suspiciously bright.

"Godspeed and good luck," she whispered as the carriage disappeared down the drive.

Lady Strickland, who had also come out to see her off, frowned at Marianne. "Why ever would Lady

Georgianna need good luck? She is returning to her family, a very respectable family I might add."

Marianne met her cold eyes. "Yes, but every journey has its hazards does it not?"

"Perhaps," she said. "What do you intend to do with the rest of your morning?"

Marianne knew that Lord Cranbourne had not yet returned from an early visit to one of his tenants, and could think of little she would enjoy less than spending time in Lady Strickland's company. "I thought I might take a walk down to the river, if that is acceptable to you?"

Lady Strickland's brow lightened. "That is perfectly acceptable, Miss Montagu. But do not wander too far, will you?"

~

Lord Cranbourne came in not many minutes later, and was not best pleased when he discovered his sister had allowed Miss Montagu to wander off on her own.

"Is this what you call taking good care of our guests?" he snapped. "Did not Lady Brancaster expressly ask you to watch over her?"

Lady Strickland eyed him in some astonishment. "Whatever is wrong with you, Anthony? She has only gone for a stroll down to the river, after all. If I did not know better, I would think your intentions towards that girl were serious!"

Lord Cranbourne surveyed her with some contempt. "You do not know me at all, Maria. Do you really imagine that I would trifle with the affections of a young lady of quality under my own roof? The very roof that once housed our mother! Do you think I could look her in the eye every time I walk into my chamber, knowing I was behaving in a manner she would deplore?"

Lady Strickland's eyes widened. "Anthony, you cannot mean it. Her father is not even a peer! Not to mention the fact that if Lord Brancaster had not been so well connected and managed to hush the whole thing up, her aunt would have been completely disgraced."

"He obviously did not manage to hush it up if you know of it," he said scathingly.

His sister coloured. "Well, these things can never be completely covered up. A few of us knew, but Lord Brancaster let it be known amongst a few of his cronies that he would be most displeased if it ever became general knowledge and he was so well respected that his wishes were observed."

Lord Cranbourne sighed. "I can see that you will not be satisfied until you have told me the whole, Maria. So, enlighten me, please. What social solecism did she commit?"

"If it will save you from making such a terrible mistake, I will tell you, even though I promised Strickland that I would not," she said. "That *woman*, eloped with Robert Pinkington. She was under age, of course, so they bolted for Gretna Green!"

These shocking facts did not have quite the intended effect. Lord Cranbourne let out a shout of laughter. "You don't say? And here they are all these years later, smelling of April and May! Why on earth did they need to do such a thing?"

"Because both parents frowned on the match, of

course. Pinkington's father, although only a baronet, was very well connected and extremely wealthy. His son had good looks, charm, and good prospects, and so it was only natural that he wished him to aim much higher than the daughter of a country squire!"

"And the country squire?"

"Just as ambitious," Lady Strickland said, in a much less sympathetic tone. "Although he did not object to his eldest daughter marrying Sir Frederick Montagu, Fanny was a diamond of the first water and he set his sights considerably higher. I blame the Gunning sisters. They planted the seed in every slightly impoverished member of the gentry, that if their child was beautiful enough they might aim as high as they pleased! Why settle for a baronet in waiting, when you might snabble a duke?"

Lord Cranbourne looked at her, a spark of amusement still lighting his eyes. "Who reached them first? The baronet or the squire?"

"The squire. Pinkington was already so rackety that I am sure his father would not have noticed his absence if he had not come home for a week. But Fanny felt guilty enough to leave a letter for her mother."

"How foolish of her," Lord Cranbourne murmured.

"I might have known you would make light of it," his sister complained. "But you have not yet heard the worst."

He raised an eyebrow.

"He did not catch up with them until the following day!" she said, with some relish. "She was brought home in disgrace, the threat of being shunned by society was held over her head, and she was persuaded to accept Lord Brancaster's very flattering and generous offer."

"Poor Fanny," he murmured.

"Poor Fanny? How can you say so? She was rewarded for her foolish, not to say immoral behaviour, by being wed to a man that positively doted on her. And now, now, she waltzes in here, as cool as you like, with the very man who nearly ruined her on her arm!"

The glint of amusement faded from Lord Cranbourne's eyes. "Enough, Maria. Although I know you will find this difficult to believe, there are more important things in this life than wealth and consequence. Have you ever considered that she has had to go through her life watching her real love playing fast and loose with other women?" He gave a harsh laugh. "Of course you have not. What would you know of love? Well you can come down from your high ropes, for I have some news for you that will be more unpalatable than all the rest."

Lady Strickland's high colour leached from her face. "Do not say that you have offered for her?"

"No. But I intend to."

The quiet tones in which he voiced this utterance, seemed to affect Lady Strickland far more than his anger or contempt had done. She sank into a chair and for once seemed lost for words.

"Not only that, Maria, but I am expecting Sir Frederick Montagu and his wife to arrive at any moment."

"No," she whispered, stricken. "I can't, I won't—"

"That is up to you," Lord Cranbourne said in a

gentler tone. "Your presence in my house satisfies the proprieties. I have already given Mrs Stevens my instructions and you may be sure they will not be housed two floors up. If you really feel you cannot face them, I suggest you retire to your room and I will inform them that you are ill."

"It will be no more than the truth!" Lady Strickland surged to her feet and fled to her chamber.

Lord Cranbourne was about to go in search of Marianne, when Wilmot informed him that there was a carriage coming up the avenue.

"Very well," he said calmly. "Alert Mrs Stevens, will you?"

The moment Wilmot left the room, he strode over to the fireplace, teased a few errant hairs into place, and tweaked his neckcloth.

By the time the carriage pulled up in front of the house, Wilmot, Mrs Stevens, and two footmen flanked him. As soon as Sir Frederick stepped down from the vehicle, he could see the resemblance to his daughter, he shared her warm, brown eyes and slightly upturned nose. He seemed at ease, in contrast to his mousy wife, whose eyes had widened in awe at her surroundings and darted about in a nervous manner.

He bowed before them and welcomed them to Cranbourne.

"Very civil of you, sir," said Sir Fredrick, smiling. "But where are you hiding that daughter of mine, eh? She will be a sight for sore eyes and no mistake."

"She is walking in the gardens, sir."

He chuckled. "She always has enjoyed taking the air. It is of no matter, I am sure you will send someone to fetch her."

"I will, of course, presently. But please come into the house."

"As you wish, young man, as you wish."

As soon as Wilmot had relieved Sir Frederick of his hat and coat, Lord Cranbourne turned to Lady Montagu.

"I am sure you wish to rest after your journey, ma'am. Mrs Stevens will show you to your room and make sure you are comfortable."

"Yes, thank you," she murmured.

He turned to Wilmot. "Bring a bottle of my best claret to the library."

"Certainly, my lord."

Sir Frederick's eyes gleamed as he took in the numerous rows of books that lined the large room. "How splendid. You put my library to shame. A man could lose himself amongst these tomes for years and never manage to read them all."

Lord Cranbourne smiled. "Please feel free to treat my library as your own, sir."

Sir Frederick laughed. "That is very kind of you, but take care not to say that to Marianne, I implore you, or I shall see nothing of her! She's never happier than when her head's in a book. Even takes them out on her rambles. I wouldn't be at all surprised if that is why she was not here to greet me. She's probably sat beneath a tree reading a novel or some poetry she has not come across before."

"No, sir. That is not the reason for her absence."

Sir Frederick raised an eyebrow but said nothing as Wilmot came in with the claret and poured them both a glass.

"Please take a seat, Sir Frederick, and I will explain."

As soon as the butler had left them, he frowned and said, "Yes, please do. For unless she has changed beyond all recognition, I do not believe that even such grand surroundings as these would make Marianne forget the duty or affection which she owes her papa."

Lord Cranbourne smiled. "I can assure you that is not the case. Miss Montagu remains very much herself, I believe. If she had known of your impending arrival, I am certain she would have been camped out on the drive in anticipation of it."

Sir Frederick took a thoughtful sip of his wine. "So, she is not aware of my visit. Go on."

Lord Cranbourne shifted a little in his chair. "She had mentioned to me how much she missed you, sir, and I wished to surprise her. I could not know that you would come, and I did not wish to disappoint her if that were the case. It was only when my man, Hintley, rode up not long before you, and informed me that you were close behind him, that I could be sure of your arrival."

"I see. It seems to me that you have gone to a great deal of trouble for my daughter, Lord Cranbourne. It would have been more usual to have sent a letter rather than send your own man."

"But not as swift, sir." He sat a little straighter, squared his shoulders, and took a deep breath. "I also had a more selfish reason for hoping you would come. I wish very much to ask Miss Montagu to be my wife, but I would not do so before I had asked your permission."

"Very proper," Sir Frederick murmured.

If Lord Cranbourne had hoped his request would be greeted with joy, he soon realised his mistake. Sir Frederick got to his feet, clasped his hands behind his back, and began to pace slowly up and down, his brow wrinkled in thought. After a few long minutes, he took his seat again and looked at his host from beneath his brows.

"I had not expected to lose her so soon," he said. "I am fully aware of the honour you do her; I am sure you could look much higher. This leads me to conclude that your heart is engaged, which I approve of. Marianne deserves to be loved. You do love her?"

Lord Cranbourne nodded. "I do."

Sir Frederick let out a long breath and then smiled. "In that case you have my permission to ask her, but I warn you, I will put no pressure on her if she does not desire the match. And I will not give my final blessing to your nuptials until I hear for myself that it is what she truly wishes."

Lord Cranbourne rose to his feet. "Thank you, sir. I shall ask her, and then I shall bring her directly to you, whatever her answer."

Sir Frederick looked amused. "You are not sure of it then?"

A wry grin twisted Lord Cranbourne's lips. "Where your daughter is concerned, I am never sure of anything."

He chuckled. "That's my gal."

Marianne was aware of a slight feeling of disappointment as she slowly strolled towards the river. The sharp anticipation that she had felt this morning at the prospect of a stroll with Lord Cranbourne had dulled. Now that she was alone, uncertainties rushed in, smothering the fragile hopes that had burgeoned in the night.

She crossed the bridge and sat by the river, watching the play of sunlight on the water and allowed its soft murmurings to soothe her doubts. She plucked a few daisies from the grass, and absently began to weave them into a chain. When she had finished, she slipped the delicate necklace over her head, closed her eyes, and despite all her aunt's warnings, raised her face to the sun.

She smiled as she became aware of the delicate symphony of birdsong that sweetened the air. But her eyes suddenly flew open as a discordant series of short barks interrupted their song. She frowned. No dog that she had ever heard barked in quite that way. Her eyes widened as she heard them again, this time followed by a shrill squeal of distress.

Marianne pushed herself to her feet and approached the riverbank cautiously. The sequence of barks followed by a squeal sounded again a little further along the river, and as she turned her head a flash of red fur caught her eye. She hurried along the bank, knelt on the grass above the spot, placed her hands flat on the ground, and slowly leaned forwards. The bank sloped quite steeply, the first few feet covered in long grass before it became a muddy quagmire.

She glimpsed the black tips of two pointed ears peeping between the long blades of grass. The squeal came again and the head turned, revealing two eyes the colour of liquid honey, beneath them a white stripe led to a narrow, slightly upturned snout.

"A fox cub," Marianne murmured softly.

The next anguished squeal goaded her into action. She sat down and eased her legs over the edge of the bank, and firmly ignoring the little voice that whispered to her of the mess she would make of her white, muslin dress, began to shuffle her way down. A huge tree shaded this part of the bank and the grass was slippery and damp, she started to slide and rolled onto her stomach, her hand snatching at a thick root that jutted from the earth.

Her feet scrabbled to gain purchase in the slippery mud and she groaned as the wet, cool, squelch between her stockinged toes informed her she had lost a slipper. She curled both hands tightly around the root, and pulled hard, finally managing to get her knees beneath her on the grass.

She turned her head and saw the amber eyes of the cub regarding her curiously. Despite her precarious situation, she smiled.

"Are you hurt, little one?" she said, softly.

The cub cocked its head as if trying to understand her, its ears alert. Then it barked and looked up. Marianne followed its gaze and saw the thick, vibrant red fur of a fully grown fox. It appeared the cub's mother had also heard its cries. She gave a sharp, raspy bark and the cub bounded up the bank and they both disappeared from view.

Marianne stared after them for a moment in silent astonishment, her eyes widening still further when two top boots took their place. Her eyes travelled up two very masculine legs, skimmed over a bottle green coat, and came to rest on a pair of amused grey eyes.

"If you fancied a swim, Miss Montagu, I could have shown you a much easier place to enter the water."

She felt the heat of embarrassment flood her cheeks. "Very amusing, Lord Cranbourne. If you have quite finished laughing at me, perhaps you would help me up?"

He reached down a hand and she grasped it gratefully, scrambling up the bank as best she could. Her colour deepened further when she stood before him and his eyes swept slowly over her from head to toe and back again.

Her humiliation was complete and she felt tears prickle at the back of her eyes. She dropped her gaze and winced as she saw the mud and grass stains that liberally smeared her gown and feet.

"I look a fright, I know," she said in a small voice.

For the second time in their short acquaintance she felt his crooked finger beneath her chin. She raised her eyes reluctantly to his, her own large in her face and shimmering with unshed tears.

"You look delightful," he murmured.

Her lips parted on a faint sigh as his eyes darkened, lit only by a small spark that glinted like the moon on a still lake. Her eyes fell to his firmly sculpted lips as they lowered towards her own with agonising slowness. Her eyes fluttered shut as they at last whispered against her own. She whimpered and swayed towards him, pressing her own more firmly against his. She heard him groan and found herself pulled against the length of his body in a tight embrace. She quivered as his tongue slid between her lips in a gesture more intimate than any she had imagined, and her hands rose of their own volition, pulling him even closer, deepening the kiss.

She swayed unsteadily, her legs trembling beneath her as he stepped away. He took her hand and held it between both his own.

"I apologise, Miss Montagu, if I have shocked you. I had only meant it to be the lightest of kisses."

Marianne blushed furiously, but replied with characteristic frankness, "I fear I must take some of the blame, sir. I really do not know what came over me."

He smiled at her in such a disturbing way that she wished he would shock her again.

"Miss Montagu, Marianne, if you were at all unsure of my feelings towards you, I hope you now understand that I adore you."

A shy smile curved her lips. "If you wish to kiss me when I look like I have traipsed through a swamp, sir, I think I can be in no doubt of it."

He raised her hand to his lips. "May I hope then, that you might not look unfavourably on the notion of becoming my countess?"

A spark of humour suddenly danced in her eyes. "That depends, sir. Can you give me your word that you will not suddenly fly into a miff whenever I displease you?"

He growled low in his throat, and briefly pulled her against him again, dropping a swift, hard kiss on her smiling lips. "No, you imp, I will give you no such promise, for I am fairly certain that I would break it. Now, put me out of my agony, will you, or will you not consent to be my wife?"

She dimpled at him. "I will, sir, but I think it most improper of you to ask me before you have received my Papa's consent."

He swept her up into his arms, grinned down at her, and began striding towards the house. "I have it. And he is now waiting, impatiently, to see his beloved daughter and hear from her own lips that she wishes to ally herself with such a ramshackle fellow as I."

Marianne gasped. "Papa is here? But how? Why?"

"Did you not say that you missed him?" Lord Cranbourne said softly.

"Oh, you did that for me, even after we had fallen out?"

"Because we had fallen out – again."

He staggered as Marianne suddenly twisted in his grip and threw her arms about his neck.

She laughed. "Oh, put me down, Lord Cranbourne, it is far too far to carry me."

"I will not put you down, you have lost your slipper, remember? And I have a desire to hear my name upon your lips. It is Anthony."

"You will be covered in mud, Anthony."

He grinned at her. "I believe I already am, so it is of no consequence."

"I suppose you are wondering what I was doing?"

"Not at all, I spied you and the fox cub before I crossed the bridge."

Marianne's brow wrinkled. "I do not understand it. It squealed as if it were in pain, yet when its mother appeared, it bounded up the bank with no difficulty at all."

Lord Cranbourne smiled fondly down at her. "They communicate by barks and squeals. The cub had probably gone down to the river for a drink and was calling to its mother to let her know where he was."

They were both still laughing when they entered the house. Sir Frederick came out of the library just in time to see Lord Cranbourne place Marianne gently back on her feet.

"Well, my dear," he smiled. "What was it this time? A rabbit that had been caught in a trap? A bird that had broken its wing?"

She ran up to him and kissed his cheek. "A fox cub, but it did not need rescuing at all, only I had already slipped down the riverbank before I realised."

Sir Frederick turned an enquiring gaze on Lord Cranbourne. "Still propose?"

"Yes, sir."

He turned back to his daughter. "You'd better take him, Marianne. It's not every one who would put up with your antics."

She smiled widely at him. "I intend to. Now I must run up and wash and change."

She turned towards the stairs and saw her step-mother hovering uncertainly on the bottom step.

"Why don't you come and help me?"

When they came down some time later, apologies had been exchanged on both sides and a few tears shed.

Wilmot came into the hall and bowed politely before her. "I hope you will not think it overly presumptuous of me, Miss Montagu, but I would like to offer my sincere congratulations on behalf of not only myself but the rest of the staff here at Cranbourne."

"Thank you, Wilmot. I do not think it at all presumptuous, and must tell you that I will depend upon you all to help me."

She had said exactly the right thing. Although Wilmot's face remained impassive, his eyes warmed. "Of course, ma'am. Your father and Lord Cranbourne are still in the library."

"Then we shall join them."

"There you are, at last," Sir Frederick said, as they entered the room. "What's all this I've been hearing about Sir Robert Pinkington hanging about your aunt like a bad smell? I wouldn't have let you go to her if I had known."

"Why ever not?" Marianne asked. "He has behaved like the perfect gentleman, and is clearly in love with Aunt Fanny. I have not seen her so happy for a long time."

"Yes, well. Whether she will stay happy is another matter."

Marianne sat down, a small frown wrinkling her brow. "I think you will have to explain it to me, Papa."

Sir Frederick looked a little flustered. "Not fit for a young gal's ears."

Lord Cranbourne came and stood beside Marianne. "I think you will find, sir, that nothing you will say will shock Miss Montagu. And as my sister has already poured the story into my ears, and I do not wish for there to be any secrets between us, I would prefer that she knew."

Sir Frederick looked at him with reluctant approval. "Oh, you would, eh? Very well."

Marianne listened to the story with great interest, never once interrupting.

"Well, my dear, what do you think of Sir Robert, now?"

Marianne smiled gently at her father. "I feel very sorry for him."

"You do? Care to explain?"

"I shall, of course," she said. "But I am surprised that I need to. Did you not marry Aunt Fanny's elder sister, for love?"

"I did," her father confirmed.

Marianne glanced quickly at her stepmother.

"Do not worry, Marianne, it is old history after all," she said quietly. "I must admit I did not feel comfortable with the frank conversations you had with your father, at first, but I have realised that they are important, to both of you."

Marianne smiled at her before continuing. "But if Mama's father had objected, would you have given in so tamely?"

"Well, no, but I was never such a wild, reckless creature as Pinkington."

"No, but you can understand why he was driven to such an extreme, surely?"

"Perhaps," he conceded. "But look at the way he has carried on all these years. He's gone to every excess…" he paused, "well, less said about that the better."

"I do not know exactly to what you refer, Papa, but does it not strike you that only someone who was very unhappy would need to behave in such a way? And think of poor Aunt Fanny. I know she grew to be very fond of Lord Brancaster, but to see her first love carrying on in such a manner, could not have been easy."

Sir Frederick looked at his daughter closely. "I have taught you to argue a point too well, I see. But what makes you think Fanny could truly forgive him all the pain he has caused her?"

Marianne looked thoughtful. "Perhaps because she understands the pain that she has caused him? Miss Bragg must know Aunt Fanny as well as anyone, yet I think that she supports his cause, in her gentle way."

"Does she now?" Sir Frederick said, surprised. "Well, I must say I have a lot of respect for Miss Bragg. She's a very sensible woman."

The door opened and Wilmot announced the subjects of their conversation.

Lord Cranbourne went to greet them. "I do hope you do not mind being shown into the library," he said. "Lady Strickland has been taken ill."

"Not at all," Lady Brancaster assured him. "Frederick!" she exclaimed. "How come you to be here?"

Sir Frederick stood and bowed to the new arrivals. "Lord Cranbourne invited me, Fanny."

Lady Brancaster, who was looking remarkably well, with a delicate pink bloom in her cheeks, suddenly clapped her hands together. "Please, tell me this means what I think it does!"

Sir Frederick smiled at her fondly. "You are as clear as ever, dear Fanny. But if you are referring to the fact that Lord Cranbourne has asked Marianne to be his wife, you are correct in your assumption."

She rushed over to Marianne and embraced her. "I knew it!" she exclaimed.

"Then you knew more than I, Aunt."

"I am very pleased for you, my dear," Miss Bragg said, smiling a little mistily at her.

"Thank you. Did you enjoy the cathedral?"

Tears suddenly brightened Miss Bragg's eyes, turning them almost transparent. "Oh, yes," she sighed. "Did I not say that I always enjoy a wedding?"

"And who were the happy couple?" Lord Cranbourne enquired. "Perhaps I know them."

Sir Robert stepped forwards and curled his arm about Lady Brancaster's waist. "You do. We are the very happy couple."

An amazed silence fell upon the room.

"I should perhaps explain that I have had a special license burning a hole in my pocket for some weeks. But every time I came close to asking Fanny to marry me, some unforeseen event would snatch the moment away. I finally decided there was only one thing I could do."

Lord Cranbourne raised an ironic brow. "Again?"

"Yes. I abducted her for a short time, with Miss Bragg's help."

Lord Cranbourne's shoulders began to shake. "You abducted Lady Brancaster with her companion in tow! You are certainly an original, Pinkington."

He grinned. "I knew her presence might be the clincher!"

"And it was," Lady Brancaster said. "I have been extremely unsure of the best thing to do. But I know that dear Aurora always knows what is best for me."

"Welcome to the fold," Sir Frederick said, shaking his hand. "But I warn you, if I see you are making Fanny unhappy, you will have me to answer to."

Wilmot, who like most good butlers did not miss a trick, had been busily filling glasses with his lordship's best claret for some moments. Lord Cranbourne gave him a nod and he efficiently distributed them amongst the guests.

"I think a toast is in order," he said, holding up his glass. "To new beginnings."

The door to the library opened and Lord Strickland wandered in, looking a little sleepy. "I say, Cranbourne, I've just had the most splendid nap, isn't it nice to have a bit of peace?" His eyes widened as he saw the throng of people in the room, all with a glass of wine to their lips. "Goodness me," he said, grabbing one of the few remaining glasses from the silver tray Wilmot carried. "Have I missed anything?"

Thank you for reading Marianne!

Thank you for your support! I do hope you have enjoyed reading Marianne. If you would consider leaving a short review on Amazon, I would be very grateful. It really helps readers know what to expect and helps raise my profile, which as a relatively new author is so very helpful.

I love to hear from my readers and can be contacted at: jenny@jennyhambly.com

Other books by Jenny Hambly

Belle – Bachelor Brides 0

Rosalind – Bachelor Brides 1

Sophie – Bachelor Brides 2

Katherine – Bachelor Brides 3

Bachelor Brides Collection

Belle is available, free, to anyone who joins my mailing list at: https://jennyhambly.com/book/belle-2/

ABOUT THE AUTHOR

I love history and the Regency period in particular. I grew up on a diet of Jane Austen, Charlotte and Emily Bronte, and Georgette Heyer. Later, I put my love of reading to good use and gained a 1st class honours degree in literature.

I have been a teacher and tennis coach. I now write traditional Regency romance novels. I like to think my characters, though flawed, are likeable, strong, and true to the period. Writing has always been my dream and I am fortunate enough to have been able to realise that dream.

I live by the sea in Plymouth, England, with my part-ner, Dave. I like reading, sailing, wine, getting up early to watch the sunrise in summer, and long quiet evenings by the wood burner in our cabin on the cliffs in Cornwall in winter.

ACKNOWLEDGMENTS

Thank you Melanie Underwood for catching the things that fell through my net!

Photo by Zhanna Karchevska

Printed in Great Britain
by Amazon